DREAMSCAPE

A Private World of Secrets, Scandals, and Schemes

William Scott Hill
Jack Horner

Copyright © 2022 Capstone Publishing LLC.

All rights reserved. No part of this publication may be reproduced, distributed, or transmitted in any form or by any means, including photocopying, recording, or other electronic or mechanical methods, without the prior written permission of the publisher, except in the case of brief quotations embodied in critical reviews and certain other noncommercial uses permitted by copyright law. For permission requests, write to the publisher, addressed "Attention: Permissions Coordinator," at the email address below.

ISBN: 978-1-7351037-5-4 (Paperback)

Any references to historical events, real people, or real places are used fictitiously. Names, characters, and places are products of the author's imagination.

Front cover image by Stephen Simon.

First printing edition 2022.

esimon@capstonepublishing.us

Capstonepublishing.us

DREAMSCAPE

II

This book is dedicated to our families who continue to inspire us.

Table of Contents

Chapter 0

"It's not as if this was a surprise.

"Damn! Even the ancient 'Internet' got this thirty years ago. The defunct World Bank predicted that by this year, 2050, the world's population would be pushing 10 billion, give or take a few hundred million. Well, they were off by several billions coz now we are at twelve. Twelve billion souls! Shit!

"Congratulations? I don't know. Don't get your panties in a wad, though.

"They say that we have come a long way as a human race. Thanks to NeuRoads, we now have NeuNet—this fantastic global network of supercomputers that miraculously and successfully interfaced with the human brain via this really tiny chip injected just behind our ears.

"You can't even tell it's there.

"What can I say? It does everything except physically wash my socks, not that I wear any.

"Tamper-proof. Haven't checked. I don't want anyone touching my ear. Hear me?

"It is my communication device, wallet, messaging system, calendar reminder, organizer, blood pressure and glucose monitor. Yeah, with my lifestyle, I need that. My health record is a command away. Controls my car, home appliances, and home security system. My whole freakin' life!

"So, let's talk about the mobile phone. Say what?!

"Ha! Some folks still carry those freakin' bricks to this day, believe it or not.

"C'mon, man. Drop those phones.

"NeuNet is the new thing.

"I just say, 'Call Mom' and my mother appears as a hologram. OK, I'm the only one who can actually see her, but who cares if I look like an idiot talking to no one?

"I do me. Period.

"It secures my apartment. It will alert me and call the cops when some clueless moron attempts to break in. Don't even think about it, you thief!

"The coolest feature is, and I hope it never happens to me, but hey who am I kidding, in the event of a serious medical emergency like, say, a heart attack, this chip will call my driverless car and rush me—fly me, actually—to the nearest trauma center while sending my vitals ahead to give the hospital a heads up.

"Listen. Peace of mind, people, peace of mind.

"And what gas emissions? Say what?! All transport, private or not, is now all electric, no exception. Solar batteries can charge while on the go.

"Wow. We really have come a long way.

"And then there is no 'money' money. Everything is 'Bits.' Yeah, words like 'cash,' 'money changer,' 'foreign exchange,' 'recession,' and 'inflation'—they got buried with the dinosaurs.

"Gone.

"Let's see ... Two Bits can get me a decent meal. A nice apartment in the suburbs is a thousand Bits per month. A two-bedroom house in the suburbs for 100,000 Bits. Living downtown, of course, will still cost you an arm and a leg. No, two legs.

"What else?

"Robot chefs, robot concierges, robot nurses, robot soldiers, robot prostitutes, driverless everything, flying cars, drone delivery, and ... spy cameras up the wazoo.

"All physical labor is now robotic. Labor? Such a quaint word. It's not missed, at all. Working because one needs to pay the bills? Well, that got old real fast. Dig this: 60% of the 12 billion get 2,000 Bits per month. 'Universal Basic Income' or 'UBI,' as they call it.

"Free money. Courtesy of an all wise and benevolent WorldGov.

"Bums and freeloaders ... in my unsolicited opinion.

"The super-rich elites control everything, like a new feudal system, and history repeats itself. Sucks!

"How long before WorldGov runs out of money? Twelve billion is a lot. You hear?

"Think about our food supply ... water? So now there is severe drought in Africa, the Middle East, and Asia. Huge charity organizations raking in billions of Bits donate bottled water to those continents. Still, people are literally dropping like flies there. Sad. No solution in sight in the near future.

"New technology has made the world safer, they say. But I can't even go to the crew-less corner store or vending machine without the authorities knowing my toilet paper brand. There are more surveillance cameras per square inch than I have pores on my freakin' body.

"They monitor everything. I wonder if they can read my thoughts. Seriously, we need a space where we can ... you know, like, talk to our friends, hang out, or just chill without being tracked. Yeah, I'll keep on dreaming until it happens. Maybe one day.

"We have given up a lot of our so-called freedom for some bullshit like safety but are we really? Safe? And from what exactly?

"Ever since the WorldGov started lording over the planet, no one, not even a Martian, is free from the intrusive machinations of the monolithic.

"A.I. created this monster and fuels it. I remember Gramps joking about Skynet getting aware. And then, it actually happens.

"Listen. The human mind is completely broken. We never anticipated the future, this present. We thought that we were on our way to paradise, but now we are at the edge of a cliff.

"Whoever thought that the explosion of information would be the actual road to hell?

"This is why I have decided to remain single. At the very least, my misery stops when I shuffle off this mortal coil. Having no offspring seems to be the most merciful thing.

"It was just a few years before I was born when the nasty coronavirus hit the whole earth. We lost friends and several uncles. Countless families worldwide lost loved ones.

"We may be due for another conflagration ... or correction. Because people do stupid things, and people never change.

"Talk about coming a long way.

"Meanwhile, we can be thankful that we still have the glorious music of the past as opposed to the garbage that the world listens to these days. Ya, ya, ya. Call me an old soul.

"But as far as I am concerned, my all-time favorites will remain: Led Zep, Aerosmith, Journey, Chicago, Earth, Wind, and Fire, Coldplay, Maroon 5, The Rolling Stones, and of course, The Beatles.

"And here is 'Yesterday' from Paul McCartney as we go to break."

Chapter 1

Sunday, July 10, 2050.
A Paris café along the Champs-Élysées.

"This is my favorite restaurant," says a young alluring Parisienne.

"I can see why," replies Rich Willard as he scoops a small portion of his Crème Brûlée dessert.

"You speak good English," he adds.

"A friend of mine teaches me."

"That's good. Any plans after lunch?" he asks.

"Not really. I was hoping we could take a walk. It's a lovely day."

"Sure," Rich nods.

A hidden earpiece on the young lady comes to life and she silently receives instructions.

"This lunch is on me," she insists, motioning for a robot waiter to approach her.

"Give me a minute," she says to Rich. "I need to freshen up. I'll see you outside."

"All units ... stand by," FBI agent Jenny Lee radios just as Rich exits the café and stands in front of the entrance.

"There you are," the young Parisienne chirps as she joins him on the sidewalk.

A white construction van and black car come to a screeching halt in front of the couple as soon as they step off the curb. Three hooded and masked thugs grab them, then shove Rich into the black car while the winsome lady is thrown like a rag doll into the van.

Rich puts up a struggle and curses repeatedly as his abductors tie him to his car seat, tape his mouth, and blindfold him.

FBI agents and elements of the French Gendarmie frantically race towards the front of the building as the van peels off and, a split second later, the black car elevates off the pavement, turns a different color, and disappears from sight.

The agents run huffing to their vehicles to pursue but to no avail.

"Fuck! Fuck!! Fuck!!!" Agent Jones yells in frustration, not relishing the fact that their asses are sure to get chewed off by the special agent in charge.

An inspector from the Police Nationale puts his communicator down and reports that drones have located the flying car.

Chapter 2

Six months before ... Friday, January 17, 2050.

Thunderous applause greets Don Goldman as he steps on the stage.

"A little over five years ago, we successfully linked the human brain with our global network of supercomputers we call NeuNet.

"Today, NeuRoads is releasing Dreamscape 2050—the most modern interactive dream world that man can come up with. Anyone in this virtual universe can meet anyone and interact in any language with simultaneous translation. With Dreamscape 2050, everything you want to experience can happen, even while you're sleeping.

"It's the private world you have always wanted."

Rock music drowns the sound of clapping as the portly Goldman leaves the stage.

He dons a bowler hat, a surgical mask, and a pair of gloves as he walks briskly for a fellow of his girth to a nearby building where he will host a special dinner for a handful of top investors.

A mean looking security team surrounds him. Heavily armed men in their 20s who would not hesitate to shoot first then apologize later if you were to even look at them askance. These fellows are not cheap, but necessary. The peons who think their present UBI's are too small have been restless lately and one can never be too sure about their intentions toward their overlords.

Don Goldman is a self-made man who grew up with his maternal grandparents after his parents divorced when he was just eight years old. His parents both died in 2020 from the coronavirus.

Though his resentment from parental abandonment never left him, he had the wisdom to make the best of what he had to become the CEO of one of the world's largest global communications and technology companies. His childhood background turned him into a shrewd but kind and inspiring leader, one who is protective of his employees. However, being a realist, Don is fully aware that he cannot please everyone.

As the CEO of a top Fortune 100 company, Don is highly respected in the business world and has extensive connections in 94 countries.

Quietly indignant at WorldGov's global control, Don envisioned Dreamscape to be a platform where people can enjoy real privacy. He shared this vision many years ago with a few trusted employees who helped him build it from scratch.

Widely known to be a germaphobe, Don does not shake hands with anyone nor allow any of his employees to see him in person. He has his own elevator in the NeuRoads Tower in Manhattan that no other person is allowed to use. While he is a world-renowned personality, he is a naturally private and highly secretive person.

Once it was conceived, the Dreamscape project was labeled "Top Secret" and was never discussed with anyone outside a small team of topnotch developers. Most of NeuRoads employees had not even heard of Dreamscape until a few days prior to today's launching.

Don personally handpicked an elite group of investors who were given only a week's notice to let go of their Bits to partially fund Dreamscape's massive global infrastructure.

Present in the gathering of investors is Rich Willard, the CEO of Willard Robotics, and his best friend, William Rivers, CEO of Crown Wines, the largest wine and spirit distributor in North America. The times do call for more liquid refreshments that make you pass out and forget.

Rich turns to Bill, "I'm glad you followed my advice and invested in Dreamscape. You won't regret it."

"You're really sure about this?" Bill asks. "How much do you really know?"

"I always do my research. I read their technical manuals. I even talked to Goldman," Rich assures him. "It's the real deal."

"I forget that you have a photographic memory, Rich," Bill nods. "I'm sure you've now got those 2,000 pages of technical specs etched in your brain. But how do you really know that Dreamscape's privacy is foolproof?"

"Bill, the Dreamscape system is self-contained, it has its own set of quantum supercomputers running its own proprietary software."

"Meaning that WorldGov can't get its dirty tentacles into it?"

"Exactly."

"Hmmm ... interesting."

Don Goldman approaches, waving his hand to greet Rich. "I am glad you could come," he says.

Rich knows Don well enough not to extend his hand for a handshake.

"Wouldn't miss it for the world, Don. Good speech."

"Thanks, Rich," Don smiles.

"By the way, this is my friend, Bill Rivers, CEO of Crown Wines. He also invested in Dreamscape, as you know," Rich says as he turns to Bill.

"Pleased to meet you, Mr. Rivers. Heard so many good things about you from Rich. Glad we finally meet."

"Likewise, Don," says Bill as he reaches out to Don for a handshake.

Rich gently pulls Bill's arm back.

"What the hell did I do wrong?"

"Nothing. I'll tell you later," Rich snickers.

"Can't wait to play golf tomorrow."

Chapter 3

Three months later … Friday, March 18, 2050, 9:00AM Eastern Time. NeuRoads Tower in Manhattan.

Everyone settles down as soon as Don Goldman enters the Board Room.

Highly advanced augmented reality and telepresence technologies enable such virtual meetings with Board members attending remotely, appearing as holograms. They know too well that Don abhors in-person meetings.

"Good morning, everyone. As you all know, Dreamscape has just reached 500 million subscribers since we launched three months ago. The math is simple. At two Bits per month per user, that's one billion Bits of revenue per month or 12 billion Bits per year," Don Goldman preens as the NeuRoads board members vigorously applaud.

Don smiles broadly and continues.

"But that is not all. Dreamscape has tremendous growth potential. The target market of Dreamscape is our NeuNet subscription base of six billion users. We are confident that we will reach the two billion mark by the end of 2050. Any questions?"

"Dreamscape marketing materials claim that this is a private virtual environment. Can you please elaborate on this?" inquires Julie Schumacher, a board member representing Prime Investment House based in Massachusetts.

"Dreamscape runs on a completely encapsulated computing environment—the fastest set of quantum supercomputers we have today. Its operating system was designed by our Chief Architect, who holds two PhD degrees from MIT. The same guy who developed our NeuNet microchip. Dreamscape runs our proprietary software. No one outside of our team has access to our code."

Julie nods, impressed.

Chapter 4

Friday, March 18, 2050, 7:00PM Eastern Time.
Home of the Willards. Long Island, New York.

"This is the Evening News. Our top story for tonight: Dreamscape subscription reaches 500 million in just three months."

At home, Rich, his wife Emily, and their daughter Margie, enjoy some Moscato as they watch the news.

"This is Dan Duran and this is your Evening News. Dreamscape CEO, Don Goldman, announced this morning that their virtual world platform known as Dreamscape has reached an amazing 500 million paying subscribers in just three months."

The face of Don Goldman comes on screen.

"How did you manage such rapid growth?" asks the newscaster.

"Dreamscape is reconnecting families and friends who have lost contact for many years. Everyone feels safe and secure in our virtual platform. Not only that. Medical researchers are now exploring possible breakthroughs with patients who suffer from neurological conditions. We will know more in the coming months," the CEO intones.

Two video testimonials of people who reconnected with their long-lost relatives in Tibet and Kazakhstan appear on screen.

"Wizard, turn TV volume to three," Emily commands. Wizard is a smart house assistant robot manufactured by Willard Robotics.

"Rich, how much did we invest in Dreamscape?" Emily inquires, clearly excited.

"About two hundred fifty million Bits," Rich replies nonchalantly.

"With the way things are going, we will most likely triple our investment in five years," he adds.

Rich Willard is a celebrity in the tech world. He is not only widely known as the CEO of the largest robotics company in the world, he also has a reputation of being a savvy investor in other high technology companies like NeuRoads.

"How much did Bill put in?" asks Emily.

"Only five million Bits. He wasn't too sure this would be a big hit. At least he followed my advice."

"Well, Bill is in the wine business," Emily remarks, taking a sip of Moscato. "Are you guys playing golf tomorrow?"

"Yes, we are."

"Dad, I know the two of you are friends but don't you get tired of each other?" Margie kids. "You play golf every weekend and you call each other almost every day."

"Hahaha. They are best friends, honey. Bill and your dad go back all the way to their MBA days at Columbia."

"And you're best friends with Bill's wife," adds Margie.

"Yeah. Liz and I go back to our high school days in Chatham, New Jersey," Emily proudly says.

Chapter 5

Bill turns to his friend, Rich, and says, "Dreamscape looks to be a monster hit."

"No doubt whatsoever," Rich replies as he grabs his driver from a humanoid caddie standing a few feet from him.

"I should have invested more," says Bill sounding regretful.

"Five million Bits is better than nothing."

"I suppose ... ahh ... you're right. Tell me more about Dreamscape."

"You know I have the microchip, right?"

"Yup. But no chips for me, you know that," Bill answers.

"I know. Anyway, this tiny computer is a NeuNet chip. It does everything that your phone does, and more. By the way, I can't believe you still carry a phone around," Rich teases.

"You told me about that chip before. So, what else is new?"

"With some AI software upgrade, Dreamscape uses this same chip to automatically log me into Dreamscape when I fall asleep," Rich explains.

"How does the chip know you are asleep?"

"The chip can pick up neural signals from my brain and vital signs like heart rate to know I've reached sleep state. It's their proprietary artificial intelligence algorithm."

"Amazing."

"So, let's just say you subscribe to Dreamscape," Rich continues, "and you get the chip. While you sleep, you are living your dreams or fantasies, as it were. All your senses are active just like when you are awake. I am not talking about an Avatar. I am talking about the real you living in Dreamscape every time that you are asleep."

"You mean I can go to London while I'm sleeping and actually experience it just like I'm there?"

"Yes, just like you are in London, except that you are not physically there, of course. So, if it is raining in London at that time, which often happens, you will actually see and experience that in real-time. Dreamscape has highly sophisticated AI engines that get real-time feeds from different sources like satellites, CCTV systems, and many others."

"Does it also mean that a person can continue to work or study while in Dreamscape?" Bill asks.

"Absolutely."

"That will be a boon for students."

"Correct."

"Can I electronically sign a contract in Dreamscape, and will that be a binding contract?"

"Ah, good question. Technically, yes. You can also access your bank account and transfer money while you are in Dreamscape."

"That sounds like a terrible idea. I don't want any of that," Bill protests.

"Well, the upside is that there are many families and friends that are being reunited through Dreamscape. Plus, there are the medical research studies that are going on to connect with patients in coma."

Chapter 6

Wednesday, May 18, 2050, 10:00AM Eastern Time.
Neurology conference in a top medical center in Maryland.

The twentysomething conference coordinator, Jill Levin, walks to the center of the stage and signals everyone that the conference is officially starting.

"Good morning, good afternoon, good evening to all of you, both in this hall and those remotely connecting from other countries. I am pleased to announce that this conference utilizes the most advanced Augmented Reality, hologram, and AI-enabled language translation technologies.*

Remote attendees can choose their preferred language and an AI system will automatically translate what is spoken to their preferred language. Remote attendees may also speak in their preferred language and the AI system will translate it to English.

"So, ladies and gentlemen, without further ado, please welcome our guest, the top Neurology expert in the world, Dr. Stephen Gallagher."

A hologram of Dr. Stephen Gallagher appears on stage. Everyone in the conference hall stands up to applaud him.

"Thank you, Ms. Levin. Good morning, everyone. We in the Neurology Research Center at Simon Institute are excited to announce a promising breakthrough in establishing connection with patients with neurologic disorders. Based on a controlled trial with 152 comatose patients, we were able to connect with 136 of them. These encounters range from a three-second visual contact to a 30-minute conversation with comatose patients. The best part of it is that we don't even have to build the technology from scratch. The platform we use is a technology that is known to many: Dreamscape."

A French news reporter, who is remotely connecting from Paris raises her hand to ask a question. She is instantly shown on the big screen.

Jill Levin calls Dr. Gallagher's attention. "Dr. Gallagher, we have a question from Ms. Danielle DuPont from France. Ms. DuPont, please proceed with your question."

As Jill speaks, the AI system automatically translates her words into French.

"Dr. Gallagher, my name is Danielle DuPont from the Paris News Corporation. This is a very encouraging development for people like me who have family members or relatives who are in coma. You mentioned that your trial involved 152 patients and that you were able to connect with 136 of them. What is the reason that some patients did not respond?" Danielle asks, while the AI system translates her words into English in real-time.

"Through a combination of advanced imaging systems and AI-powered analytics engines," Dr. Gallagher explains, "we were able to detect neural paths that may be blocked. That's the hypothesis we need to test. The good news is that there are drugs that are currently on trial that are specifically targeted to reactivate those types of neural pathways. We have initiated discussions with pharmaceutical companies to establish protocols for research collaboration."

A news reporter connecting from Japan, Hidehiko Matsumo, raises his hand. His face shows up instantly on the big screen.

Jill Levin calls Mr. Matsumo's name and gives him a queue to ask his question.

"Dr. Gallagher, this is Mr. Hidehiko Matsumo from the Tokyo Daily News. My question is this: have you found any indication that this microchip from NeuNet may have any negative effects on humans?"

"Thank you for your question, Mr. Matsumo. There have been a number of studies around that area.

"What comes to mind is a research paper from Dr. John Lieberman that was published in October last year. Essentially, there has been no established connection between the NeuNet microchip and neurologic disorders reported by 22 consumers of the NeuNet chip. Dr. Lieberman's team also ran their data for analysis using the most advanced AI platform we have today. However, Dr. Lieberman believes that they will need more data to perform a more meaningful analysis to establish correlation, if any."

Chapter 7

Wednesday, May 18, 2050, 7:00PM Eastern Time.
Home of the Rivers family.

"This is your Evening News. Our top story for tonight: Top Neurology expert announces breakthrough in connecting with comatose patients." Music kicks in.

"Good evening. This is your news anchor, Ron Martin. And this is our top story for tonight: Top neurology expert, Dr. Stephen Gallagher, from the Simon Institute announced this morning a breakthrough in connecting with patients stricken with neurologic conditions."

A video excerpt from the Neurology conference appears on screen showing Dr. Gallagher reporting, "Based on a controlled trial with 152 comatose patients, we were able to connect with 136 of them. These encounters ranged from a three-second visual contact to a 30-minute conversation with comatose patients. The platform we used is a technology that is known to many: Dreamscape."

"Liz, did you hear this news about Dreamscape?" Bill Rivers shouts over the TV audio from the living room.

"Yes, that's a replay, honey. I saw that this afternoon," replies Liz as she walks in from the kitchen.

"This is awesome! This is sure to boost Dreamscape's stock price," Bill exclaims.

"I know. I was just thinking of my Aunt Mary in Texas who has been in a coma since December. Could there be a chance I can connect with her through Dreamscape?" Liz wonders.

"No microchips for us, remember," Bill reminds her.

"I know, but this ... changes everything," Liz argues.

"We can talk about that later. By the way, where is our son?" Bill asks.

"Jude went straight to his room right after dinner," says Liz with a sigh.

"I noticed that he's been disappearing right after dinner for several weeks now. Do you know what's happening? He's been sleeping much earlier than usual," Bill remarks worriedly.

"Brace yourself," Liz turns to her husband. "Jude signed up with Dreamscape. He has the chip."

"What? How did that happen without my knowledge?" Bill asks, his voice rising.

"Your son is now an adult. He's 19. He doesn't need your approval, Bill," Liz answers gently.

Chapter 8

Bedroom of Jude Rivers.

"Wizard, play Johann Sebastian Bach's 'Air in G.'" As the AI system plays the Baroque classic, Jude slowly drifts into sleep and enters Dreamscape.

"I want a bouquet of a dozen red roses," says Jude. Suddenly, he is holding a bouquet of roses just as he imagined.

"Take me to Lucile LeMont," he commands in his sleep. And, in a heartbeat, he is standing in front of his Dreamscape friend, Lucile, who has been waiting for him while strolling around Place de la Concorde in Paris near the Luxor Obelisk.

Lucile can barely contain her excitement to see Jude. This is their 18th meeting in Dreamscape since they first accidentally crossed paths in that virtual world three weeks ago.

Jude was then a new subscriber of Dreamscape and was looking forward to exploring different cities. While he considers himself a seasoned world traveler and has physically been to over 30 countries—thanks to his wealthy parents—Paris remains his favorite city.

He was in Dreamscape walking along the Champs-Élysées when he first saw Lucile in a pink dress trying to cross the street. At first sight, the lovely and charming Lucile immediately tugged at his heartstrings. He was completely captivated by her beauty that all that he desires now is to see her again and again. He realizes that despite all the riches that he can enjoy, it's Lucile that truly makes him happy.

Jude claims that he saved Lucile's life when he grabbed her hand to keep her from being flattened by a speeding car. Lucile retorts that no such thing happened because she is a bright-eyed no-nonsense young lady who has complete control of herself and her surroundings.

Now, on their 18th meeting, Lucile pulls Jude's hand, calling out, "Let's go and see the Alps!"

In an instant, they are at the foot of the Alps. They muck about for hours as they chat about the things they do in their waking hours.

"I'm out of school," Lucile shares. "I work as a waitress in a café along the Champs-Élysées. I have to earn to support my younger brother, Pierre, and my sickly mother."

"Don't you have other siblings who can help you?" asks Jude.

"I have an older sister, who left when our father died four years ago," Lucile murmurs, tearing up.

"I am so sorry, Lucile. How old is your sister?"

"My sister will turn 25 next month," says Lucile. "I haven't spoken to her since she left," she adds.

"What do you do?" Lucile smiles at Jude.

"I study at LaGuardia High School in Manhattan. I major in fine arts."

"You have a major in high school?" asks Lucile, her right eyebrow raised.

"Oh, yeah. LaGuardia is the top arts school in America," Jude explains. "You audition to enter LaGuardia and you have to show that you excel in all your subjects."

"You must be very smart." Lucile is impressed.

"I don't know about that," Jude grins.

Chapter 9

Monday, May 23, 2050.
Principal's office, LaGuardia High School in Manhattan.

The Fiorello H. LaGuardia High School of Music & Art and Performing Arts in Manhattan is a highly competitive school. Aside from having excellent grades, students have to audition to demonstrate extraordinary talent in music, art, or the performing arts. Their roster of graduates includes some of the most prominent names in the music, Broadway, television, and film industries.

The academic calendar ends in late June. So, it comes as a surprise to Emily Rivers that the school principal wants to meet with her in person with just a month to go before classes end.

"Mrs. Rivers, I am Dr. Meredith Saunders, principal of LaGuardia High School. Please have a seat."

Liz suddenly feels a bit perturbed as she takes a seat.

"Mrs. Rivers, I want to talk to you about your son. Jude is one of our best students at LaGuardia. He is also top in our fine arts program. Jude has so much potential," Dr. Saunders begins.

"Thank you, Dr. Saunders," Liz replies, adding, "Jude was valedictorian in elementary and middle school."

"Without a doubt, Mrs. Rivers. The reason I requested this meeting with you is because we want Jude to succeed," the principal's tone turns serious. "However, he has to do his part."

"What do you mean, Dr. Saunders?"

"Well, Jude has been missing deadlines for his assignments and art projects for close to three weeks now. Here is a list of homework and projects that he missed."

"Now, this is the first time we have seen this happen," Dr. Saunders adds. "Is there anything that you may have noticed with Jude lately?" she inquires with concern.

Chapter 10

Wednesday, May 18, 2050, 10AM Eastern Time.
FBI Office in Manhattan.

It is another sunny day in spring when one would expect to hear birds chirping as they perch on tree branches. The calming music from these winged creatures has been all but silenced, though, as flying cars now dominate the skies. These AI-powered vehicles rudely waggle tree branches as they zoom by.

Progress has its price.

The Director of the Federal Bureau of Investigation, Will Bridges, looks through his office window to watch aeromobiles zip through the skyline. He puts down his coffee mug to begin another briefing of his team of agents.

His phone rings just as he sits down.

"Yes, Ma'am," he speaks curtly after listening for a few minutes and rings off. The VPOTUS was not the type for chitchat. Her reporting line to WorldGov is a bittersweet cup and their constant nudging for intel has been a pain in her neck.

"Dreamscape," Bridges begins, "has been gaining a lot of public attention. I'm ordering Cybercrime to start looking at this. I want to know if there are criminal elements using the platform."

"And ... I want weekly updates that I can send to the VP."

Kit Sharper, head of the Cybercrime Unit nods.

"I'll put Jenny Lee and Luke Jones on it."

"Rookies. Thought that they were on Rainwater?" Bridges queries.

"We've discussed this before, Will. You know we had a string of retirees. Lee and Jones may be rookies, but they're top of their class. Sharp techies. Sharp shooters. Completed our boot camps with flying colors, both."

Just in their mid-twenties, Jenny Lee and Luke Jones are viewed as greenhorns in the bureau. But any Fed officer will attest to Kit Sharper's track record of hiring the best agents in the organization. Trained on advanced cybersecurity, criminal investigation, and military tactical operations, Lee and Jones are top graduates of the academy.

Jenny Lee may be gifted with a supermodel frame, but she is no barbie doll. Born in a military family with her father and three brothers serving in the special forces, she grew up playing toy soldiers, planes, and plastic swords and guns. It comes as no surprise that Jenny is a champion black belter and has uncanny familiarity with a broad range of military weapons. On her third year in computer engineering at Stony Brook University, she signed up for an internship at the bureau. It didn't take Kit Sharper an hour to spot the next rock star in the Cybercrime Unit. Though constantly surrounded by men, Jenny does not fall prey to sweet talk. Tightly guarding her security and privacy, Jenny lives on the 7th floor of an apartment building in downtown Manhattan with her pit bull named "King."

Luke Jones, on the other hand, is a product of a broken home. At a tender age of nine, he has already seen the ugly face of marital infidelity worn by his gallivanting father. Learning from his bruises, Luke swore to himself that he will be a loving and faithful husband. His childhood trauma led to a natural aversion towards men, especially married men, who show attraction to his adorable fiancé. Luke's outstanding record in track and field was his ticket to a full scholarship in the computer science program at the State University of New York at Albany. He then joined the agency's highly competitive internship program.

Jenny and Luke consistently landed in the top two in theory and practical exams administered by the agency. That also means pinpoint accuracy in hitting multiple fast-moving targets.

"I know. I know," Bridges nods.

"I'm bumping Mike Yoder to Rainwater. Will be a good fit as he has a master's degree in Chemistry" replies Kit.

"OK then," the Director dismisses the cyber head.

Chapter 11

Wednesday, May 18, 2050, 6PM Eastern Time.
Home of the Rivers family in New Jersey.

One pleasant thing about spring is that the sun is still high at 6PM. Moving towards summer, one can enjoy more evening hours before moonrise.

Families who spent winter cooped up in their homes can't wait to use their outdoor grills for a nice barbecue.

With all the wealth that the Rivers family has accumulated, such fun get-togethers are a rarity. Their 245,000-Bit custom-designed backyard with a fountain and gazebo has been sitting unused for over a year. Money can't buy happiness, they say.

Despite his busy schedule, Bill does make an effort to find time for his son, Jude.

Jude has always been an A student. So, the news from the high school principal is quite disturbing, to say the least.

"It is time for a serious chat," Bill tells Liz.

Knocking on his son's bedroom door, Bill calls out, "May I come in?"

"Hey, Dad," Jude replies warily.

"How are you doing?" Bill inquires, picking up Jude's Calculus textbook from the floor.

"Not too bad," Jude responds with a slightly nervous tone.

"Sorry that I've not had the chance to check up on you for ages."

"Yeah, right," Jude says in his head.

"Your mom met with your school principal the other day. Dr. Saunders says that you've been missing assignments and projects," Bill suddenly blurts out.

"Crap!" Jude mutters, as he tries to hide his anxiety attack.

"Jude, you are expected to graduate at the top of your class," Bill says, clearly irked.

"Dad, get off my case," Jude replies, obviously annoyed.

"What do you want to do with your life?"

"Dad, it's not as if I dropped out. I just want to take a vacation. Like go to Paris."

"You're grounded!"

"What?!"

"If you weren't on Dreamscape every freaking day…" his father starts.

"I know what I'm doing. I am 19 years old," Jude retorts as he stands up and leaves the room.

Chapter 12

Friday, May 20, 2050, 6:30PM Eastern Time.
Home of the Willards in Long Island, New York.

The mansion of billionaire Rich Willard is a showcase of the most advanced robotics and automation technologies that money can buy. After all, he is the chairman and president of Willard Robotics, the world's leading provider of humanoids, robots, robodogs, and a broad array of security and automation solutions.

The home of the Willards is equipped with a highly sophisticated home security system, a dozen humanoids and 20 robodogs that guard his perimeter fence 24x7, robot cleaners, and robot chefs that can cook any dish that the Willard family can imagine; not to mention the most modern hologram system, entertainment system, and his fleet of 18 self-driving and flying cars from some of the top automotive companies in the world.

His few closest friends have been on board Rich's three 260-foot mega yachts, each vessel having three decks with generous living spaces, a theater, swimming pool, gym, and spa. Each luxurious yacht is loaded with highly advanced communications equipment that can connect him from anywhere out on any sea.

Rich also owns two Bombardier jets that fly him and his family to concerts or ballet shows in other states or countries whenever they find some extremely rare free time.

"Thank you for cooking, honey. That steak was really good!" Rich gushes to his wife, Emily.

"You're welcome, hon."

"And thank you, chef," Emily laughs as she points to their state-of-the-art robot cook, the D7000.

"Anything scheduled tonight?" she asks her husband.

"Not really. I want to go to bed early. Golf with Bill tomorrow," Rich replies, stretching.

"Some tea before bed?"

"Yup." Rich's automatic reply is like a muscle reflex action, while his mind travels elsewhere.

The D7000 silently whirs away to do Emily's bidding of serving chamomile tea.

Rich steps out of the shower and is putting on a robe as Emily hands him the cup of tea.

"Here you go, honey. Let me just check on Margie and I'll join you," Emily says.

"Margie OK?" Rich inquires.

"Yeah, just want to say good night to her," Emily speaks over her shoulder.

Emily comes back to find Rich snoring away.

Rich appears in Dreamscape and is wandering around Central Park in Manhattan.

It is a warm evening and the sun is still up.

A young French lady falls from a bicycle. A slim five-foot-seven-inch Parisienne, she could easily pass for a top model. Her refreshing and innocent-looking face can soften the heart of any human being.

"Oh, you poor thing," thinks Rich as he runs to the damsel in distress and offers his hand to help her get up.

Chapter 13

Friday, May 20, 2050, 8PM Eastern Time.
Dreamscape.

Gone are the days when people went to malls for shopping or dining. Malls have become extinct due to this global paradigm shift that started some 30 years ago favoring online shopping. Young people say it is a complete waste of time to walk inside a building just to look for things to buy. Nowadays, anyone can shop and buy anything using the global neural network.

What is more amazing is that, with Dreamscape's highly advanced technology, one can "virtually try on" any dress or shirt, look at oneself in a mirror, and decide whether to buy the item or not.

Buying an item in Dreamscape is as simple as saying the words, "I want to buy this." Dreamscape will automatically order the item, charge your bank account, and arrange for delivery.

Other than shopping, people feel that Dreamscape is a safe haven for them to connect with their family, friends, and colleagues away from the watchful eyes of WorldGov. Some privacy, at last.

"Anything unusual?" asks Lee as she and Agent Jones stroll in Dreamscape ... inside Central Park.

"Nothing so far."

"Hey, look at what we have here!" Jones exclaims, nudging his fellow agent.

"That must be Rich Willard ... the billionaire," rejoins Lee.

"Interesting," Jones muses as he takes a mental note of the sighting.

Chapter 14

An apartment in Paris.

The smell of cappuccino fills the morning air as a robotic coffee maker prepares two cups for a couple of apartment dwellers somewhere in Paris.

Meanwhile, a robot chef cooks breakfast made of three eggs over medium and warms three croissant rolls.

The robot chef sets the breakfast table for two with fancy plates, matching cutlery, and two glasses of orange juice.

"Good morning." An attractive young lady wakes up and greets the man beside her.

"I finally met Willard in Dreamscape," she adds.

"You mean Rich Willard?" the man is immediately interested.

"Yup."

"The same guy in the photo I showed you last week?"

"Positive."

"The Big Boss will be happy." The man grins devilishly. "Good work. Keep me posted."

Chapter 15

Saturday, May 21, 2050.
Golf course.

"How are things in your part of the jungle?" Rich asks, as the driverless golf cart quietly whisks the golf buddies to the 8th hole.

"Business is picking up in North America," Bill replies as he shakes his head, ruing the fact that more people have turned to drinking their misery away.

"You don't seem too excited about making more money. How's family?" Rich asks.

Bill remains silent for a second before responding.

"Liz is worried about Jude. He's spending way too much time in Dreamscape. He's started to neglect his studies. Never happened before."

"Sorry to hear that. Dreamscape ... is a drug, the ultimate high," Rich says matter-of-factly.

"You are not helping."

"I didn't mean to be unsympathetic, Bill. But you invested in Dreamscape. Why don't you try it?" asks Rich.

"No chipping me, you know that," Bill protests.

"Just saying that you may get an insight on how you can manage issues with your son," Rich replies, hitting the ball and watching it land in a lake.

"Shit! Not again," Rich shakes his head and throws his golf club to a humanoid caddie in a childish tantrum.

"Terrible shot," the humanoid caddie unwittingly exclaims.

Rich glares at the robot and quips, "Hey, watch your mouth, you dummy. Who programmed you?"

"Willard Robotics."

"Fuck you!" Rich exclaims as he knocks the head off the humanoid.

Bill is not surprised at this outburst. He has known Rich, who was born with a silver spoon in his mouth, to have a dark side, much worse than a bad temper, even back in their MBA days.

To Rich, only successful business people, multi-millionaires to be exact, are worth his time. Everyone else is a second-class citizen.

Rich hates immigrants, completely ignorant of the fact that his own ancestors migrated from Europe to America in the late 1800s. At times, though, Rich would selectively remember his ancestry, tracing back to some European royalty that went into exile after being driven out by a military coup.

His concealed delusions of nobility thoroughly persuade him that he is invincible, a high and mighty lord anointed by the universe and to whom everyone should bow down.

True to his reputation as a very shrewd businessman, Rich fires 20% of his workforce every year to keep all his employees up on their toes. He calls it "the most effective motivational strategy."

Oblivious to the plight of the needy, Rich holds on to his principle that it is immoral to donate to charity as it only promotes indolence. He is proud to tell anyone about this "guiding philosophy in life."

Chapter 16

Monday, May 23, 2050.
FBI Headquarters.

Monday morning meetings are not exactly a welcome event for many, especially after a busy weekend. However, great coffee and bagels with Philadelphia cream cheese have a way of quickly turning things around.

"Someone forgot to order half and half, but we have French Vanilla in the fridge," says Kit Sharper as he walks towards the mini refrigerator in a corner of his office.

"Go ahead, Lee, don't let me stop you. Let's hear your update."

"Thanks, Kit." Lee addresses the group around the table inside the office of the FBI Cybercrime Unit Head. "LeMont and Rich Willard are an item in Dreamscape."

"Willard Robotics?" asks one of the agents.

"Yes. Big fish ... and I smell something, well, fishy," Kit Sharper says as he raises his eyebrows.

After an hour of mind-numbing reports, Kit dismisses the group. "Back to work, boys and girls."

As everyone files out, the Unit Head gives a voice command to his communicator, "Call the FBI Director."

A hologram of Will Bridges appears in front of Kit Sharper.

"Confirmed. LeMont is in Dreamscape. Recently sighted with billionaire Rich Willard," reports Kit.

"What's the connection?"

"Don't know yet. We will find out."

"I will inform VPOTUS," Director Bridges affirms tersely.

Chapter 17

Around noon, Manhattan bustles with driverless cabs picking up random passengers. Some folks prefer to walk to nearby restaurants for lunch. It's good exercise anyway.

Bill Rivers has a different agenda that day. He is psychologically preparing himself to do something he wished he never had to do. He spent all morning exercising mindfulness and all the other crap that his therapist taught him to do, but he still feels very uneasy about this. It's against his beliefs.

"You will hardly feel a thing, Mr. Rivers," assures Dreamscape store manager, Dana Fontain, as she prepares a disclaimer for Bill to sign.

"Please sign here," Dana says pointing to a section on her monitor, which is nothing but a borderless, transparent sheet of shatterproof glass.

"We will apply a topical anesthetic before we inject the chip."

"Whatever. Let's do it."

"If you need any help in any of the Dreamscape functions, all you need to say is 'NeuNet, I need help.' Then specify the function," Fontain says calmly.

"I am technically illiterate."

"You will be fine, Mr. Rivers," Dana replies.

"This chip is designed for all levels of users. We can't all be rocket scientists, Mr. Rivers," Dana adds with a small smile.

"Now, how do I log in?" asks Bill.

"The microchip has AI-powered technology that will sense when you are asleep and will automatically log you into Dreamscape," Dana assures him.

"And don't forget, this chip also serves as your phone. You don't have to carry that thing you are holding, Mr. Rivers," Dana chuckles as she points to Bill's archaic rectangular communicator.

"How?" Bill asks.

"Just say, 'Call home' or whoever it is you want to talk to.

"The person you are calling appears as a hologram in front of you that only you can see or hear," Dana explains. "Highly secure, too."

"Won't that be dangerous when I'm at the wheel?" Bill asks.

Dana is incredulous as she realizes that the guy in front of her still drives his car when most automobiles are now AI-controlled self-driving vehicles.

Managing not to roll her eyes, the salesperson answers, "Well, you can easily direct the call to your car audio by just saying 'Connect this call to my car' and the call will redirect to your car's audio system."

"Nice!" says Bill with a wide grin.

Chapter 18

Thursday, May 26, 2050. Noon time.
A high-end Japanese restaurant in Manhattan.

"How have you been, Emily?" Liz Rivers asks, taking a bite of yellowtail sashimi.

"Oh, not too bad. Business is good. A lot of orders for eldercare robots. Rich is looking into France for expansion," Emily Willard replies as she raises her hand to catch a robot waiter's attention. Waiters are all the same, robots or otherwise, she thinks to herself.

"What's with France?" Liz inquires.

"Aging population, I guess. I wouldn't mind flying to Paris every now and then."

"Oh, Paris? Absolutely!" Liz agrees.

"How's your family?" Emily asks.

"Jude has been spending too much time in Dreamscape. I'm concerned that he is losing focus, especially on school. Know anything about it?" Liz asks as she sips saké from a dainty cup.

"Very little except it seems to be an excellent investment. I really don't like the idea of having anything foreign in my body, though," Emily frowns.

"Yeah ... I feel the same way. But, this new breakthrough with patients in coma makes me wonder about my Aunt Mary in Texas," Liz shares.

Chapter 19

Saturday, May 28, 2050.
An abandoned warehouse somewhere in Europe.

For two decades now, global logistics companies have taken over the world's supply chain, leaving behind a significant number of empty warehouses across Europe that were formerly owned by small independent operators. Warehouse laborers became part of the unemployment statistics as robots replaced humans across many industries.

Unknown to many, however, some of the abandoned warehouses have been taken over by gangs that carry out illicit activities. They are usually considered "small fry" to local police authorities, who don't even bother to track them as they are a complete waste of time ... until they become a significant threat to the community.

On a cunningly quiet Saturday morning, three driverless trucks, each tugging a 40-foot container, park inside an abandoned warehouse. Their registration plates identify them as originating from Belgium and Poland.

Three solar-powered drones hover above the warehouse like eagles watching over their nests.

Robots lift crates from one corner of the warehouse to a staging area near the containers.

Humanoids—robots that move like human beings—scamper about making sure that each crate goes into its designated container.

The crates are labeled "RAINWATER CHARITY."

Chapter 20

FBI Director Will Bridges rolls up the blinds in his office. The early morning sun is out in force. He looks out the window and gazes at the tree-lined boulevard. Despite the idyllic view, he finds himself thinking that the glass windows in his corner office can stop anti-tank rockets.

His thoughts are playing back his grueling foxhole experience some three decades ago when Kit Sharper, FBI Cybercrime Unit Head, walks in. Bridges doesn't even hear the knock on the door.

"Coffee?" offers the Director.

"No, thank you. I've already had my caffeine dose for today," Sharper grins.

"It looks like a harmless mix of ground beans and hot water, but caffeine makes it so addicting," Bridges thinks aloud.

"Well, water futures are through the roof, even higher than coffee beans," Kit interjects. "The world thought that potable water was unlimited. We were wrong. Now, the drought across half the globe makes it even more catastrophic."

"Without water, we're doomed," Will mutters, gazing into his cup of joe.

"Speaking of water," his tone turns earnest as he taps his tablet. "Rainwater is a charitable organization based in Europe. Donates free bottled water to poor areas in many countries. Operates a medium-size desalination plant. Funds hydroponics projects. Completely automated. And no one has seen the head of Rainwater, no trace of his whereabouts, digitally or otherwise," Will explains, still fiddling with his smart pad.

"Exactly. And they're in WorldGov's radar ... because?" Kit's voice trails off.

"The organization's financials, their public postings, do no match their global reach. The math doesn't add up. They publish a donor list of a few tens of thousands, each giving a few Bits a month. I mean, bless them, but the rest of the world has been suffering from donor fatigue ... can't blame them.

"So, Rainwater must be funding their operations through some other means. They are just way too secretive for their own good. Almost like they're hiding something. Does not pass my smell test. I'm curious as to why they do what they do, especially giving away a scarce commodity like water. I want to know."

"On it, boss!" Kit says as he makes his way out.

Chapter 21

Tuesday, May 31, 2050.
An abandoned warehouse somewhere in Europe.

The three autonomous trucks leave the warehouse in a convoy.

Many people still find it quite eerie to see trucks that seem to have a mind of their own. These self-driving trucks are able to park, drive on side streets, find alternate paths to avoid traffic, cruise on highways, and locate their destination anywhere in the European continent.

However, technology is not perfect. Any of the three trucks can break down anytime, or worse, be hijacked.

To mitigate such risks, an intelligent drone lifts up from the same location and follows the three trucks. It sends updates to a home base somewhere in Paris.

About thirty minutes later, a new set of three self-driving trucks arrives at the warehouse. With clockwork precision, robots stage crates next to the empty 40-foot containers.

Three black drones continue to circle the sky above the warehouse. Closely watching the area.

Chapter 22

Tuesday is usually a long day for Bill Rivers. It is the day when he gets reports on how his multi-million-Bit company performed during the prior week.

Liz is intimately familiar with Bill's calendar so she prepares dinner a bit later on Tuesdays compared to other days of the week.

"Good night," Jude says curtly, as he leaves the dining table and sprints to his bedroom.

"Have you heard from Principal Saunders?" Bill asks his wife, pouring a perfectly aged Bordeaux into his wine glass. Undoubtedly an expert in fine wines.

"Nothing, Bill. You see how your son rushes to his bedroom after dinner ... every night?" Liz seethes.

Then, she follows through, "Found anything yet?"

"Are you kidding? Liz, I've only been in Dreamscape for two nights. I have zero knowledge on this damn thing!" Bill laughingly exclaims.

Chapter 23

Wednesday, June 1, 2050.
Dreamscape.

"Great to see you again," Rich says as they stroll through Central Park.

"Nice to see you too, Mr. Willard," the young, alluring LeMont replies as she lightly touches the back of Rich's arm.

"It's Rich."

"OK, Mr. Rich," she replies.

They both giggle.

Observing from a few yards away are Jones and Lee.

Surrounded by a group of loud tourists, the incredulous Bill Rivers is watching the same thing!

"Rich, it's my birthday next week," she reveals with a coy smile.

"When?"

"June 12."

"Really? Mine's this Friday," Rich says excitedly, like a 10-year-old.

"Hmm. Will you ... celebrate ... with me, what I mean is ... in Paris ... in person?" she flirtingly asks.

"Ah ... yeah, why not?" replies Rich, throwing all caution to the wind.

She smiles as she gently squeezes his hand.

Rich looks around.

Chapter 24

Thursday, June 2, 2050.
Breakfast table in the Rivers family home.

By early June, spring starts to turn to summer. To many students from well-to-do families, summer means grand vacations. For others who may not be so fortunate, it is just another season, like other seasons, to work and earn more Bits.

For seniors like Bill and Liz Rivers, there's another reason to celebrate.

"Invites from Emily for Rich's birthday party tomorrow night," Liz announces.

"Cleared my calendar after 3PM. Is there anything you need me to pick up?" Bill asks his wife.

"Well, get your best friend a present," Liz says, her eyes rolling.

"Well, what gift do you give to a tech billionaire?" Bill replies, his mind relentlessly nagging him of what he had seen in Dreamscape. In Central Park.

Chapter 25

For many decades, the Port of Rotterdam has been a showcase for automation. It is likewise known to be the busiest shipping port in Europe.

In the last ten years or so, the Rotterdam Port has been completely unmanned—a fleet of automated cranes and container-handling equipment outfitted with advanced artificial intelligence capabilities has rendered human labor unnecessary.

Today, June 2, 2050, seems like just another day at the port. Without any homo sapiens intervention, three self-driving trucks zip through the port's automated gates built with countless CCTV cameras, motion sensors, x-rays, and a highly sophisticated OCR system that can read container numbers with 100% accuracy.

Three AI-guided straddle carriers equipped with GPS and collision detection technologies approach the trucks and lift the 40-foot containers from their trailers. The containers are then whisked off somewhere in the port's vast container yard.

The trucks and trailers exit the port as quickly as they came in. A drone continues to watch over them as they travel to their next destination.

Chapter 26

Friday, June 3, 2050.
Home of the Willards.

Limousines and exotic sports cars with vertical takeoff capabilities line up on a long driveway that leads to the grand entrance of the Willards' mansion.

Only top socialites and the global who's who make it to Rich Willard's guest list. No press people are ever invited to his parties. While Rich is a celebrity in the tech world, he has hyper allergy or, to be more precise, severe paranoia when it comes to paparazzi. He would shamelessly volunteer in any conversation his unfounded theory that the press is itching to destroy him.

Names of guests are announced as they enter the grand lobby of his stately home.

Once the celebration begins, Rich beams and waves his arms as if conducting his guests as they sing him a "Happy Birthday."

"Thank you all for coming and for making my 60th birthday very special," he booms as they toast him with glasses of champagne raised.

"Now, drink yourselves silly," he says, pauses, then laughingly adds, "in moderation of course."

Everyone laughs.

The guests break into small groups as everyone works the room.

Rich pulls Bill aside and asks, "I'm going to Paris next weekend. Care to join me?"

"I can't. I have prior commitments," Bill replies, his eyes a little leery.

"You're turning down my invitation?"

"You know me, Rich. It's just that I need to attend to some personal matters."

"Too bad. I thought you'd be interested," Rich is disappointed.

"What's with Paris?" Bill tries not to sound too interested.

"What do you mean? Paris is Paris."

"Of course. Just asking."

"Oh, I'm thinking of possibly setting up a satellite office there," Rich declares, waving his hand to greet other guests.

Chapter 27

Friday, June 10, 2050.
Paris international airport.

Rich Willard disembarks from his private jet with a small 10,000-Bit leather duffel bag. A seasoned globe trotter travels light.

He dons his sunglasses, a sports coat, and his signature cap as he steps into the airport terminal. He navigates the area like it's an extension of his manor. Within a few minutes, Rich is out of the building.

"Happy birthday to you and me."

"So happy you could come, Rich."

The young Parisienne hugs Rich tightly as a driverless cab that he ordered purrs to a stop in front of them.

They get in, oblivious to a drone that has been quietly cruising overhead.

While she holds Rich's hand and tells him of her planned itinerary for their rendezvous, the driverless cab navigates through Paris traffic like a master maze solver.

They arrive at the Ritz Paris where they check in.

"I can't believe you are here," the young seductress whispers as she plants a kiss on Rich's lips.

Rich swiftly looks around, then smiles at her. He despairingly tries to hide his bewilderment.

Chapter 28

Saturday, June 11, 2050.
An abandoned warehouse just outside Paris.

A masked man walks forward and back inside a warehouse while talking to an unseen person.

From a distance, the man may appear to be mentally unstable. But just a few steps closer and anyone who hears the witty exchange is sure to be amazed.

Meanwhile, humanoids guard the exterior walls of the warehouse while two drones fly over the building for reasons known only to its owner.

"Good work, Dima. Good work," a man's voice is heard over the PA system.

"I aim to please," Dima purrs.

Locals can easily tell from their accents that the two are not native to Paris.

Chapter 29

Sunday, June 12, 2050.
Home of the Rivers family.

Liz Rivers looks at her husband in disbelief. She cannot believe what Bill just told her.

"That's why Rich is in Paris today. I saw them in Dreamscape and heard their plans myself," Bill says as he comes clean to his wife about what he witnessed.

"I don't know, Bill. Wasn't it ... just a dream? It happened in Dreamscape, right?"

"No, it wasn't just a dream. It was real."

"Are you sure?"

"You don't understand how men think," Bill retorts.

"Well, yeah. I don't understand how you can think of your best friend that way. He would not do that to Emily!" Liz protests. "You are completely wrong, Bill, sorry."

Bill had never had such a heated argument with his wife in the thirtysomething years of their married life. He is not about to make this day miserable because of a matter that doesn't even pertain to his own family.

Bill looks at Liz and says in a calm tone, "I guess you're right, honey."

Chapter 30

Monday, June 13, 2050.
FBI Headquarters in Washington, D.C.

"Yoder has an update on Rainwater," Kit Sharper reports as he and Yoder appear as holograms in front of FBI Director Will Bridges.

"Seems like a significant portion of their free water goes to Africa, which kinda makes sense because of the drought there. They have a small field office in Mogadishu that serves as the main hub for the continent. The Middle East and Asia are likewise beneficiaries of their charity. Both hard hit by the global drought," Yoder narrates.

"True, but expensive high-tech operation," Kit adds.

Yoder continues, "They do have a presence in Europe but it's confined to the Greater Region. They are headquartered in Antwerp but that office is mainly staffed by robots. Still trying to talk to an actual human, but no luck."

"How about their CEO?" asks Kit.

"Robert Devall didn't return any of my calls. Not sure if I got the right number."

"Any leads as to why they are skittish about their financials?" Bridges butts in. "It's almost as if they're hiding something."

"Or we are dealing with a nerdy recluse. What do you think, Yoder?" Kit interjects.

"All I know is that the Devall family dominated the bottled water industry for decades. Who knows? This charity work may just be their way of giving back."

"Convince me." Bridges insists. "Something doesn't make sense."

Chapter 31

Monday, June 20, 2050.
Willard Robotics Headquarters.

At the top floor of the Willard Robotics global headquarters in midtown Manhattan is a massive board room equipped with the latest telepresence technologies capable of delivering lifelike holograms and real-time translation for over a hundred languages.

"Sales are up by 10% in the last quarter. Our marketing campaign is making a dent and we are optimistic that this is sustainable for the next four quarters," Rich Willard is all confidence as he addresses the Board of Directors.

"My trip to Paris last week went well. It would be good to set up a satellite office there to give us a bigger footprint across the pond," he adds.

A chirp in his ears alerts him to an urgent inbound email. He glances at his handheld device and immediately turns pale as he sees pictures of him and the gorgeous Parisienne kissing.

"Everything OK, Rich?" Evelyn, his second-in-command whispers in a concerned voice.

The question snaps Rich out of his sudden dread. He manages to mutter, "Oh, I'm fine. Just a bit jet lagged."

His heart is racing as he excuses himself to use the restroom.

"My VPs will answer any questions that you may have. Thank you, all. Kindly excuse me."

Chapter 32

Monday, June 20, 2050.
An abandoned warehouse just outside Paris.

"Good work. We got Rich Willard by the balls," the masked man gloats as he rests his arm on a young lady's shoulders. "He must be in severe panic by now."

"How much do you have in mind?" the lady asks.

"Oh ... three million Bits for now."

"Cheap. That's peanuts for a billionaire."

"Exactly. He won't risk bad press for some loose change."

"I don't know how much longer we can do this," she cautions.

"It's for a good cause."

"Get real."

Chapter 33

Willard Robotics Headquarters.

He ... she ... or they had sent an untraceable message made of letters cut out from random magazines along with the pictures.

Willard is shaking as he reads. The message goes straight to the point.

"Transfer 3 million Bits to account J98-K345YKL by June 23 or photos go to paparazzi."

"Stupid! How could I be so stupid!? Shit!"

Rich is still mentally kicking himself when Bill calls.

"Where are you?" Rich blurts out.

"Why? What's up?" Bill replies.

"I need to speak to you."

"You sound dead serious. Sure."

"I'll come find you," Rich says.

"All right."

Chapter 34

Rockefeller Center.

"Someone is trying to blackmail me."

"What the hell!?" Bill exclaims.

Rich unloads everything to his friend who listens incredulously as the details come out.

"Why!? This is bullshit! What the fuck were you thinking, man?!" Bill is trying not to yell.

"I could lose everything, Bill. Everything! I'll be ruined," Rich groans as he covers his face with his hands.

"How do we know that this bastard won't go public even after you pay up?" Bill hisses.

"I ... don't know," Rich seems resigned. "But I gotta take care of this right away."

Chapter 35

Thursday, June 23, 2050.
Somewhere in Paris.

It's summer and Parisians are basking in the afternoon sun.

Tourists, both in small and large groups, stroll around and marvel at the art in every nook and corner of the city.

A glamorous young lady's in-ear communicator beeps.

"Willard just sent it," says the man on the other line.

"Three million?"

"Exactly."

"Nice," she smiles as she strolls along the Champs-Élysées, holding hands with a European tycoon.

"Keep up the good work."

Chapter 36

Friday, June 24, 2050.

Breakfast table at the Willards' home with Rich, Emily, and their daughter Margie.

"You OK, hon?" Emily asks Rich. "You seem kind of zoned out."

Rich is picking at his food. He looks up flustered. "Ah ... sorry, hon, just thinking about stuff at work."

"Good to know it wasn't my cooking." Emily teases.

"Oh no, no ... this spread is ... delicious," Rich hastily assures her.

Margie rolls her eyes.

"By the way, there was a 3 million Bits withdrawal ... from ... our account," Emily remarks.

"Oh, sorry. I forgot to tell you. I thought I'd put in some money for a robotics startup in Paris."

"From our personal account?"

Chapter 37

Friday, June 24, 2050.
Ritz Paris Hotel.

A sophisticated-looking robot in the lobby of a five-star Paris hotel welcomes an enchanting young lady and a visiting Middle Eastern mogul as they get out of a self-driving limousine.

They walk straight to the front desk while a robot porter handles the travelers' suitcases.

Moments after check-in, she gazes into the man's eyes, holds his hand, and kisses him passionately.

Intelligent digital cameras are mute witnesses to everything, the super cloud ingesting every detail.

"Bingo," the man recording the event quips, as the song "Another One Bites the Dust" rings inside his head.

Chapter 38

Friday, June 24, 2050.
Home of the Willards.

The doorbell rings.

Margie walks in from the dining room and answers the door.

There are two agents holding up identification.

"Agent Lee and Agent Jones from the FBI. May we speak to Mr. Richard Willard?"

Rich walks up to the door.

"How may I help you?"

"Mr. Willard, we would like to ask you a few questions. Could you please come with us to our office?"

"What's this about?"

"Your recent trip to Paris. We just have a few questions."

"Can you give me a few minutes? By the way, can you please write down your office address?" Rich asks.

Agent Jenny Lee nods and writes on a piece of paper. "We'll just wait out here."

"Thanks," Rich responds.

"Emily, can you please call Atty. Brighton and ask him to meet me at the FBI office? Here's the address," Rich instructs.

Chapter 39

Home of the Willards.

Emily Willard feels a sudden wave of panic as she tries to sit on a couch in their living room.

She has had a few episodes of anxiety attacks over the last several years and learned from her psychiatrist how to pace her breathing. She tries hard to distract herself from focusing on her tachycardia by thinking of happy thoughts, but her efforts meet no success.

She wanders aimlessly around the house. The three-story Willard mansion suddenly feels like a prison cell. Trepidation grips her as she steps into the kitchen. Perhaps a cold drink will calm her nerves. She takes a few sips of water, puts down the glass, then looks at it wondering if she had taken a sip. She can't stop the flood of thoughts and questions rushing through her mind.

"What is happening?"

"Why is the FBI talking to Rich?"

"How can I help Rich?"

"What will happen to us now?"

"I need help."

"Who can I talk to?"

"Who can I trust?"

As she struggles to find answers, there is one name that pops up in her mind: Liz Rivers, her high school best friend.

Emily calls Liz, her voice shaking.

"Liz, I need to talk to you. It's urgent!"

"Do you want me to come over?" Liz senses her friend's panic.

"Please," Emily implores.

Chapter 40

Friday, June 24, 2050.
Interrogation Room inside the FBI office in New York.

"Mr. Willard, your recent remittance of 3 million Bits to account J98-K345YKL. Can you confirm this?" asks Agent Lee.

"Can you please explain what this is about?" Atty. Brighton breaks in.

"Mr. Willard's business transactions are confidential," he protests.

"Mr. Willard, what is your relationship with Juliette LeMont?" Lee presses on, ignoring the lawyer.

"What has Mr. Willard's relationship with this LeMont ... got to do with this?" the lawyer asks in objection.

"Why don't you just let Mr. Willard answer that question?" Lee says as she turns to Rich.

"Juliette is a friend," Rich says quietly.

"How long have you known her?" Jones asks.

"Around five years," Rich says as he stares at the table top, hoping to conceal his lie.

"Where did you meet her?"

"Sorry, but you don't have to answer any more of their questions, Mr. Willard," Atty. Brighton stresses, now overtly pissed with the interrogation.

"Again, why don't we just let Mr. Willard answer the question?" Lee replies.

"I don't remember. Maybe in one of my trips to Europe many years ago. Then I met her again recently. In Dreamscape," Rich admits dully.

"Are you telling the truth?" Lee inquires with a stern look.

"Objection!" quips Atty. Brighton.

"You recently flew to Paris to meet with Ms. LeMont," Jones proceeds.

"Leading statement," objects Brighton.

"I'm just asking Mr. Willard to confirm."

"I flew to Paris to explore business opportunities."

"What business opportunities?" asks Jones.

"Robotics, my global business," explains Rich.

"Business? Your remittance came from your personal bank account."

"Nothing wrong with that. I invest in startups using my own money."

"The Interpol has been on Juliette LeMont's case for some time now," Lee explains.

Rich's eyes widen in alarm. "She's an entrepreneur," Rich stammers. "What has she done?"

"Are you being blackmailed, Mr. Willard?" Lee cuts to the chase.

"I object! That's a leading question," Brighton protests.

"Atty. Brighton, Ms. LeMont is not engaged in any registered business in France or anywhere in the world. We suspect that she may be connected with an extortionist group. Victimizes ultra-rich people. But, no one wants to talk," Jones explains.

"Shitloads of Bits are changing hands and seem to be heading in one direction. Strangely, none to LeMont's personal account," adds Jones.

"She works for an organization," Lee says.

"What organization?"

"We aren't sure yet, but we will find out soon," Lee's tone is firm.

Rich winces at this.

Chapter 41

Friday, June 24, 2050.
Home of the Willards.

In the deep valleys of life, we look for people we can trust. People who will not judge us. People who will walk beside us throughout the entire journey. At times we find that in the company of a high school friend.

Liz Rivers rings the doorbell.

Emily Willard opens the door and hugs her friend.

"So glad you're here," Emily says as they walk to the living room.

"What happened?" Liz's eyes are wide.

"The FBI picked Rich up to answer questions, Dean Brighton is with him."

Liz looks at her friend intently and quietly asks, "Anything unusual with Rich that you noticed recently?"

"Nothing really. Except that he took a trip to Paris two weeks ago and then transferred three million Bits from our personal account," Emily replies.

"Did he say what for?"

"He said it's seed money for a start-up company there," explains Emily.

"Did he say what company?"

"No."

"Oh ... sounds fuzzy," Liz shrugs.

Emily suddenly bursts into tears.

Liz comforts her friend of many years, "Rich is a savvy businessman. I'm sure everything will be fine."

Even as she says this, Liz can't help but feel guilty that she had instantly dismissed Bill's narrative on Rich's reckless exploits.

Chapter 42

Friday, June 24, 2050.

Hours after the interrogation, Rich gets a call from Agent Lee.

"Hi, Mr. Willard. How are you?"

"I am doing fine. Thank you for asking."

"Would you have a few minutes to meet with us here in our office?"

"Do I need to bring Atty. Brighton?"

"I don't think that will be necessary."

"OK. Give me an hour."

Rich Willard's Benz aeromobile vertically lands in front of the FBI Tower. He enters the building and Agent Lee leads him to a small conference room.

"Mr. Willard, we believe you are innocent," Agent Lee explains.

"I am!"

"But we need your help," she promptly adds.

"Juliette LeMont has been seen in the Belvedere Hotel in Dreamscape these past two days."

"Here is an opportunity to get to the bottom of this," Jones breaks in. "That is, if you agree to help us."

Lee and Jones look at the billionaire with bated breaths.

Rich remains quiet for a moment and then nods, "Sure, why not."

Chapter 43

"Rich Willard," Juliette exclaims, clearly very surprised to see Rich at the grand lobby of the Belvedere Hotel.

"Oh, hi, Juliette! How are you?" Rich asks as he tries to look pleasantly amazed at the sight of her.

"Busy with business since we last met," Juliette explains. "So, what brings you here?"

"Want to personally check out this spanking new seven-star hotel, like six wasn't enough."

"I know, right?" rejoins Juliette.

"We have an upcoming global convention for our top robotics customers. This is the perfect venue," beams Rich as he looks around the lobby.

Rich lowers his voice as he grapples with an attempt to appear candid. "By the way, I'm flying to Paris on July 9. Want to meet up?"

"Absolutely," Juliette replies with a Mona Lisa smile.

Chapter 44

Sunday, July 10, 2050.
A Paris café along the Champs-Élysées.

"This is my favorite restaurant, Rich," the seductive Juliette LeMont enthuses.

"I can see why," replies Rich as he gently scoops a tiny portion of his dessert, a Crème Brûlée.

"By the way, your English is good."

"A close friend in Paris has been teaching me."

"That's good. Any plans after lunch?" asks Rich.

"Not really. I was hoping we could take a walk. It's a gorgeous day," Juliette beams.

"Sure. Actually, I can use some fresh air," agrees Rich.

Meanwhile, plain-clothes agents position themselves within a few hundred meters from the café.

"Everybody, on your toes," Agent Lee instructs a team of combined FBI, Paris Police, and INTERPOL agents saturating the area. Agent Jones stands next to Agent Lee as they both swiftly scan their surroundings for possible surprises.

A hidden earpiece on Juliette comes to life and she silently receives instructions.

"This lunch is on me," she suddenly insists, motioning for a robot waiter to approach.

"Are you sure?" Rich inquires gently.

"Of course," she says patting his hand. "Give me a minute. I need to freshen up. I'll see you outside."

"All units, be on high alert," FBI agent Lee radios, just as Rich exits the cafe and stands in front of the entrance.

"There you are," Juliette chirps as she joins him on the sidewalk.

"What a beautiful day," Rich says.

Suddenly, a dirty white construction van and a black car come to a screeching halt in front of the couple as they step off the curb. Three black hooded and masked thugs grab them. Two shove Rich into the black car, while Juliette is thrown like a rag doll into the van.

Rich puts up a struggle and curses loudly like a child in an uncontrollable tantrum as his abductors tie him to his car seat, tape his mouth, and blindfold him.

FBI agents and elements of the French Gendarmie frantically race towards the front of the building as the van peels off. A split second later, the black car elevates off the pavement, turns a different color, and disappears from sight.

The huffing agents run to their vehicles to pursue but to no avail.

"Fuck! Fuck!! Fuck!!!" Agent Jones yells in frustration, not relishing the fact that their asses are sure to get chewed off by the special agent in charge.

An officer from the Police Nationale puts his communicator down and proudly assures the outraged agent, "Drones operated by the French Police have been able to track the flying car. We know exactly where they landed."

French Agent Jean Palace looks at Agent Jenny Lee. They nod at each other with a smile.

Chapter 45

An abandoned warehouse just outside of Paris.

An autonomous flying car decelerates, hovers, and lands vertically amidst the high grass of the field. It then drives itself into the warehouse where six armed humanoid robots appear and surround the vehicle.

They roughly pull the blindfolded Rich from the car and force him to the ground.

"You think you can fool us!" growls an angry voice from out of the darkness.

The voice sounds somewhat familiar to Rich, but acute panic blurs his memory.

After a moment, the voice roaringly continues, "Go back to your home country ... tonight ... and stop seeing the girl!"

Rich can only moan helplessly as an armed humanoid slams his face against the cold concrete. Never has he been so humiliated in his life.

In his terror, snot flows from his nose as he hyperventilates.

"If you still want to see your family ... leave Paris ... tonight," the disembodied voice drones as Rich struggles against the unrelenting strength of the robot.

A renowned expert on humanoid soldiers, Rich personally architected a good number of these robotic marines. It is not a remote possibility that this merciless 350-pound machine could be one of his more recent creations. Talk about having a dose of your own medicine!

While relieved that his abductors will let him go, Rich trembles at the tormenting thought that he has lost control over the safety of his family.

"Don't try anything stupid, Rich-o!" the vaguely familiar voice threatens ominously.

Chapter 46

Outside the abandoned warehouse.

"This is the police!"

The deceptive serenity of the night is violently broken as armed men come running out of the tree line to take up positions around the building.

"You are surrounded! Come out with your hands in the air!" a megaphone barks out the orders.

In a wink of an eye, humanoids rush to the windows and start firing at the small army of law enforcement agents. The initial volley from the metal thugs immediately takes down two cops.

Return fire from the gendarmes puts a robot out of commission.

A number of officers frantically drag their wounded comrades out of the line of fire as sparks from bullets and loud ricochets fill the dark night.

Meanwhile, back inside the warehouse, a group of masked men violently drags Rich to a deep blue flying car on standby. The brutal scuffle that breaks out with the billionaire rips one of the men's masks and exposes his face to the scarred and beaten captive.

A group of agents barge in from around the corner and yell, "Freeze!"

The warehouse gang immediately opens fire and the cops respond with their own barrage.

The masked men sprint to two vehicles leaving Willard behind, clutching his left belly in pain. He groans as he realizes that he has been shot. He passes out at the sight of his own blood.

Jones and Lee rush to Rich's side. Lee calls for an ambulance as she notices the pool of blood around the unconscious body.

Chapter 47

Monday, July 11, 2050.
A large hospital in Paris.

"Mr. Willard, you are very lucky," the French surgeon announces. "That bullet ripped some flesh from your left side but missed major organs. So, for now, you need to rest and recover."

Rich musters just enough strength to nod.

The doctor's voice fades out in Rich's mind as he gets overwhelmed by rapid replays of his own near-death experience.

"What the hell did I just get myself into?"

The surgeon steps out as FBI agents Lee and Jones enter the room.

"Mr. Willard, the French police will guard your room 24x7 until we can get you out of here and sort things out. Until then, try to relax and get some sleep," Agent Lee advises Rich.

"In the meantime, we have detailed men to secure your house Stateside round the clock," she adds.

Rich can only softly mumble his thanks.

Chapter 48

Wednesday, July 13, 2050.
Rich Willard's hospital room in Paris.

While his body is recovering from the bullet wound, Rich's mind remains sharp as ever. With what little strength he can gather, he quietly issues a command to his NeuNet chip, "Call Bill Rivers."

"Bill, are you alone?"

"Yup, in my office, what's up?"

"I am in a hospital in Paris. I was shot," Rich quietly reveals.

"What the hell!" Bill exclaims.

"I'm OK," Rich explains hastily. "I'll survive, I think."

"Does your family know?"

"No. Keep this to yourself for now ... please," Rich pleads.

"OK." Bill sighs deeply. "Take care of yourself, Rich. I'll see you when you get here."

Chapter 49

**Thursday, July 14, 2050, 3:15AM Paris time.
Rich's hospital room in Paris.**

A French policeman on guard duty looks up as a masked male nurse with a tray enters Rich's room.

The man carefully puts the tray down on the bedside table so as not to awaken Rich. He quickly draws a hidden pistol from his scrubs, points it at the sleeping patient ... when suddenly a swiftly gliding robotic nurse assistant enters the room and startles the unwanted visitor. Sensing the danger, the French cop guarding the door acts on his initial suspicion that this particular nurse is up to no good.

The policeman's flying kick makes contact with the arm of the assassin who drops his gun. Then, a forceful blow sends him crashing into the infusion pump. The violent commotion rouses Rich whose first instinct is to roll off his bed, out of harm's way.

The assassin quickly gets to his feet and scampers out the door with the cop in hot pursuit.

The chase abruptly ends when the policeman runs head-on into a hover gurney on its way to the morgue.

Chapter 50

Thursday, July 14, 2050, 7:32AM Paris time.
Rich's hospital room.

Several police inspectors chat in the corridor while a detective interviews the charge nurse.

Billionaire Rich Willard is lying on a hospital bed with monitors and IV tubes attached to his body. He lies stuporous with his eyes half open, struggling to make sense of the bustle around him.

Intense hunger and thirst leave him with no energy to even open his mouth and ask for food and water. Shielded from the pains of poverty, Rich submits to a humbling realization, "This must be how poor people feel."

His mind is a cacophony of confusion, severe anxiety, regret, anger, and fear for his family's safety. That violent mix of emotions is further stirred by something he was half expecting.

"Mr. Willard, we need to bring you home as soon as possible," Agent Lee's voice breaks in. "Paris is just not safe for you right now."

Rich closes his eyes and nods in agreement. His thoughts rush to questions he wishes he had answers to.

"What will Emily say?"

"What will Margie say?"

"What will my board of directors say if they find out?"

"Is my family safe?"

"Who are these gangsters who tried to kill me?"

"What organization do they work for?"

"Why target me?"

"What have I done?"

"Am I safe?"

"I have to first make sure I can get home alive."

"How?"

As his thoughts travel at lightspeed, Rich finds comfort in Agent Jones's words.

"We will fly with you. Arrangements are being made as we speak."

"The Sûreté are all over this building," Jones assures him, "and will provide escort until we are safely on board your private jet."

Chapter 51

Paris airport.

An airport porter pushes a wheelchair towards Rich as he is helped out of a car.

Agent Lee and Agent Jones stand close to Rich while they scan the surroundings for any signs of danger.

Suddenly, two gunshots are heard and mass hysteria ensues.

Shouts of people and cries of babies heighten the pandemonium.

The sniper just misses Rich as the latter suddenly stoops down to pick up his small duffel bag.

Agents Lee and Jones promptly scan the surroundings to trace the trajectory of the fired shots.

Realizing the situation, the sniper rushes aboard a flying car that suddenly vanishes from the sight of the two FBI agents.

"Let's go," Agent Lee directs tersely as she wheels Rich into the airport building. Lee's trained eyes had caught the panic-stricken airport porter crawling his way into the terminal building during the commotion. "Can't blame the guy," she ponders.

"Agent Lee, we will take care of this," assures French police officer, Pierre Chapelle. "Our squad is following the sniper. You have to go."

Accompanied by three French police officers, Rich Willard and the FBI agents breeze through airport security.

Chapter 52

JFK airport.

The eight-hour flight from Paris to New York feels like forever to Rich. He tosses and turns on his private jet's luxurious seat. He painstakingly attempts to calm his nerves and comfort his mind to get some much-needed sleep. But a sharp memory is both a blessing and a curse. Trauma is never easy to brush off. It sneaks into one's consciousness with no warning, no rhyme, nor reason.

As his Bombardier lands at JFK in New York, Rich's heart rate races to the top. An anxiolytic can only do so much.

Agent Yoder meets Rich, Lee, and Jones at the gate. "How are you, Mr. Willard?" he asks.

"I am much better. Thank you for asking," the billionaire lies.

"I know you're still recovering, Mr. Willard, but I am sorry to break this news to you," Agent Yoder's tone turns kinder and calmer.

Rich's hands shake and his eyes twitch as he struggles to steel himself.

"Mr. Willard, your daughter, Margie, has been abducted."

Rich Willard groans audibly as the news hits him like a punch to the gut.

Chapter 53

Home of the Willards.

Fifteen FBI and NYPD high-speed aeromobiles park in front of the Willard mansion as Rich and the agents arrive.

Emily rushes to meet her husband as soon as the door opens.

"Someone kidnapped Margie! What's going on, Rich?" Emily frantically asks as her husband tries to comfort her.

"Are you alright? Why are you limping?" she asks in panic as Rich's injuries become apparent. Rich attempts to look calm and composed, but he quickly realizes that Emily is quivering in abject terror.

Rich tries to find the words, but his natural business eloquence escapes him. With knees buckling and head bowed, he succumbs to complete devastation from the horrible events that have happened to him and his family.

"Mrs. Willard, your husband needs rest," Agent Lee gently reminds her. "We will try to answer all your questions."

Emily composes herself and helps Rich to their bedroom. A few minutes later, she rejoins the agents in the living room.

"We will do everything to get your daughter back, Mrs. Willard," Agent Jones assures the visibly distraught billionairess.

Emily breaks down in tears as she shows Jones the abductor's ransom note.

"Transfer 10 million Bits to account J98-K346YKM by July 15 or Margie dies."

Chapter 54

Friday, July 15, 2050.
An abandoned warehouse in New Jersey.

Ten hover squad cars carrying FBI agents and New Jersey SWAT swoop silently down on a nondescript warehouse near the seaport.

As the agents and cops disembark from the vehicles, they are immediately met with rapid gunfire from four strategically positioned humanoid soldiers, forcing everyone to eat dirt.

One of the SWAT members uses a directed EMP rifle and the ruthless machines succumb to death by frizzling circuits.

The SWAT team and the FBI agents enter the warehouse, hyperalert and ready for more surprises.

In a dark corner of the structure, behind one tall pile of crates is Margie Willard. She is alive but almost catatonic from shock. Her hands and feet are tied, and her mouth is covered by thick packaging tape.

"You're going home," one of the cops says.

Margie weeps uncontrollably.

Chapter 55

Monday, July 18, 2050. 6:30AM.
Home of the Willards.

The Willards gather around the kitchen island unaccompanied by their usual breakfast mood. Lifting a fork is drudgery. No amount of food could give them enough energy to wrap their heads around their tragic string of misfortunes. No place is safe, they now realize, despite their massive wealth and elaborate home security system.

"Blueberry pancakes?" Emily quietly offers to break the deafening silence.

Margie wipes her tears as Rich tries to comfort her. He cannot gather the courage to look at Emily in the eye.

At such a time as this, Rich knows that the best response is silence.

Chapter 56

Rich calls his robot executive assistant to clear his calendar for the day. He then boards his Aston Martin flying car and heads for the FBI office for an incident review and debriefing.

"We are glad your wound is healing fast," Agent Lee greets him with a smile.

"We appreciate you taking the time," she adds. "This shouldn't take long. We just have a few questions."

"Anything else you remember from Paris? Any details that you recall?" the agent gently prods Rich.

"The shock of it all kinda mushed my brain. Honestly, being shot is something that ... that ... I never imagined ... would happen ... to me," Rich's voice begins to break, the recollection makes his hands shake uncontrollably. He looks out the window.

Agent Lee remains silent.

"The really weird thing ... about it ...," Rich's voice trails off, "the strangest thing is that the voice called me 'Rich-o.' No one has called me by that name since grad school."

"I mean ... only Uri." Rich ponders that realization.

"Uri who?"

"Uri ... Uri ... Borstin."

"Who is this Borstin fellow?" Lee asks.

"I'm not saying that he is the guy. It just struck me that ... I had a classmate...who used to call me 'Rich-o.' The only one ... who called me ... by that name. Uri Borstin, my classmate in Columbia MBA," Willard's words come slowly. "I believe he went on to get two post docs in MIT, specializing in artificial intelligence and cryptography."

"How sure are you about this?"

"Ah ... hmm ... sure? Not 100%."

"I caught a very quick glimpse of one of the guys and he did look a bit like Borstin. It's been decades but ... he ... sure ... he sure looked like Uri. I mean a thinner version of Uri. Maybe not exactly Uri ... or maybe it's not Uri ... or someone who looks like Uri ... I don't know," Willard shudders.

"Agent Jones, I want everything on this guy, Uri Borstin," orders Cybercrime Unit Head Kit Sharper.

"No! Wait. What?" Rich protests.

Chapter 57

Monday, July 18, 2050, 11:30AM.
Home of the Willards.

"How are you, honey?" Emily gently asks her daughter.

"I'm not sure, Mom. Can't sleep," Margie responds in a shaky voice.

"Margie, you know you can tell me anything, right? I am your mom. I love you."

"I know, Mom. Love you, too."

"We are arranging for you to see a therapist," Emily pulls her daughter into a hug.

Margie's eyes begin to tear up.

Chapter 58

Monday, July 18, 2050, 12:30PM.
FBI Cybercrime Unit Office.

"Strange ... Uri Borstin's digital footprint is almost non-existent except for the fact that he is ... or he was ... the Chief Architect of Dreamscape," Agent Jones reports to the head of the Cybercrime Unit, Kit Sharper.

"I'd say he does not want to be found," adds Jones.

"Hmmm. That is strange."

"Well, either that or some people don't have time for idle chitter-chatter."

"There's one way to find out. I will ask Will Bridges to contact Dreamscape Head Office and formally request for information on Uri Borstin," Sharper says after a thoughtful pause. Kit knows very well that he will be up against the head of a giant corporation.

"Might be a long shot, Kit. Don Goldman is well-connected," Agent Jones replies.

"I know."

Chapter 59

Monday, July 18, 2050, 2:20PM.
A Japanese restaurant in Manhattan.

"Rich, you are either the luckiest man or the most unfortunate son of a bitch!" Bill exclaims sotto voce as Rich absently pushes a solitary piece of sushi around on his plate.

"I can't believe the shit that has dropped on you ... what happened to you? You bloody son-of-a-gun," Bill sputters as he realizes he is beginning to sound like Rich with his cocky rhetoric. Perhaps Bill subconsciously wants Rich to get a measure of his own trash talk. Bill then picks up a fork to end his existential struggle with a pair of chopsticks.

"Yeah, I know," Rich mumbles as he leans back in his chair and gazes at some empty space.

"How do you really feel?" Bill probes.

"I feel like a piece of shit. Worst in my whole life."

"I bet."

"At least my wounds and bruises are healing fast," Rich desperately consoles himself.

"By the way, do you remember ... Uri ... Uri Borstin from our MBA days in Columbia?" Rich tries to sound casual.

"Who will ever forget a guy like that Uri?" Bill recalls. "He topped every class and made all of us look like dim-witted dropouts."

"Weirdo, though, not much of a talker. I didn't like it when you told me that he called you Rich-o. I mean I wouldn't want people calling me Bill-o," Bill adds.

"But you're OK being called Billy?"

"Well, yeah. What's wrong with that?"

Rich rolls his eyes in disbelief.

"OK. Anyway, he's the guy," says Rich.

"What do you mean?" Bill asks, his eyebrows arched.

"Nothing. Just a random thought," Rich shrugs.

"Oh, come on, Rich, what's with Uri?"

Chapter 60

Monday, July 18, 2050, 3:00PM.
Dreamscape. Office of the CEO.

"Don, you have a call from the Director of the FBI, Will Bridges. Line 2," Don Goldman's robot assistant announces.

"I'll take it," Don answers as Will Bridges appears as a hologram in front of him.

"Hi, Don. Good morning. Thank you for taking my call."

"I have a meeting in 10 minutes. How can I help," asks Don warily, as he tries to grab his teacup.

"We want to ask your Dreamscape technical team a few questions," Will goes on.

"Do you have a warrant?"

"We're not making any arrests, Don," the FBI Director retorts. "We're just gathering data."

"Then you are investigating."

"We're just gathering data."

"Then the answer is 'No'," says Don as he gestures to terminate the call.

"Wait. We have reason to believe that an international group of extortionists and blackmailers is using Dreamscape to victimize people," Will cuts to the chase.

"What our subscribers do inside Dreamscape is none of our business," Don frowns. "I have to go. I need to prepare for my next meeting."

"One of the victims is a major investor of Dreamscape," Will Bridges presses on.

"Who?" Goldman challenges.

"I can't give you the name. Look, we're here to help protect your investors and your business."

After a long pause, Don says, "Talk to our Tech Lead, Roger DeKalb. I'll let him know."

"I will send two of our agents, Agents Jenny Lee and Luke Jones."

After the talks with Don Goldman, Director Bridges calls Kit Sharper.

"Kit, we got green light. Contact Dreamscape Tech Lead, Roger DeKalb. By the way, keep an eye on Don Goldman. He holds his Dreamscape cards very close to his chest."

Chapter 61

Tuesday, July 19, 2050, 10AM.
Dreamscape Head Office.

The office of the Dreamscape Tech Lead, Roger DeKalb, is one that you would expect from a hyper nerdy techie. Automated door opener using three-factor authentication: voice recognition, iris recognition, and finger scanning, plus the most advanced monitors, plus surveillance cameras, plus augmented reality gadgets, plus telepresence equipment, plus robot assistant. And most important of all, a robotic coffee machine that makes the best caffè lattes and cappuccinos one could ever have.

In contrast to Roger with his ultra-modern and well-kept office, the tech lead is a work junkie who often forgets to wash up or brush his salt-and-pepper hair.

"Agent Jones from the FBI. This is Agent Lee. We just have a few questions," says Agent Jones to Dreamscape Tech Lead, Roger DeKalb.

"Don told me. But what the hell is this about? Am I in trouble?" Roger asks testily.

"No. We're just gathering information. Our director cleared this with your CEO," Lee assures.

"I know. Got a call from Don."

"We just have a few questions. May we proceed?" asks Agent Jones.

Roger nods, half convinced.

"What is your job here at Dreamscape?" the agent proceeds.

"Am I being investigated?" Roger is wary again. "Did I do anything wrong?"

"No. You're not being investigated," Agent Jones insists.

"I am the Tech Lead. Meaning, I manage the technical teams that look after the global computing infrastructure of Dreamscape."

"Do you manage the software, too?" Agent Lee digs in.

"No."

"Who is in charge of the Dreamscape software?" asks Agent Lee.

"Uri. Uri Borstin. Chief Architect of Dreamscape," Roger replies.

"May we talk to Uri Borstin?"

"Good luck. No one knows how to get hold of him."

"How come?"

"He reports directly to Don. Most of our tech employees work from home."

"What's Uri's address?"

"We are not authorized to give any employee information to anybody."

"We are not just anybody."

"I know, but what you are asking is confidential information."

"We will keep this information confidential."

Roger looks at Agent Jones and Agent Lee.

He thinks to himself, "What will be the risk of giving Uri's address to the FBI? Do I need to escalate this to Don? I guess it won't hurt to give them Borstin's address."

He pauses for a moment and then gestures to access the Dreamscape employee directory.

"I'm not even sure if this is updated," Roger admits as he hands them Uri's address.

Soon after the government men leave his office, Roger DeKalb calls Don Goldman and reports, "They didn't ask anything about our global infrastructure. They want to talk to Uri Borstin."

"Did they say why?" Don asks.

"They seem to be more interested in our software."

"Well, good luck to them. I haven't even seen Uri myself for years now. Keep me updated."

Chapter 62

Wednesday, July 20, 2050.
FBI Cybercrime Unit Office.

"This is all we got from Dreamscape: an address in Syracuse," reports Agent Jones to FBI Cybercrime Unit Head, Kit Sharper.

"Syracuse, New York?"

"Yes. Most Dreamscape tech employees work remotely."

"Who supervises Uri?"

"He reports directly to Don Goldman, the president of Dreamscape."

"Hmmm ... interesting. Don Goldman."

"Anyway, check out Uri in Syracuse," instructs Kit Sharper as his phone rings. FBI Director Will Bridges appears as a hologram in front of him.

"We got an update from the French, Kit," the Director begins. "That warehouse in Montreuil just outside of Paris where Rich Willard was taken is operated by Rainwater. I will send you a copy of the report."

"Rainwater? The charity organization ... Interesting," Kit comments with eyebrows raised.

"That's right, Rainwater. Looks like more than just a charity organization," Will Bridges goes on.

"More interesting info. Rainwater operates with robots. Rich Willard is the CEO of the largest robotics company in the world. Something fishy here, Kit."

"Talking about Rich Willard ... he sounds certain, well, not a hundred percent, but he thinks that Uri Borstin, the Chief Architect of Dreamscape, has something to do with his abduction. They were classmates in Columbia MBA," Kit says matter-of-factly.

"Why would Uri abduct his former classmate? What's the motive?" Will ponders aloud.

"Good question. And where does Juliette LeMont fit in this puzzle?" asks Kit.

"Exactly. And did Don Goldman order Rich Willard's abduction?" adds Will.

"Is Uri Borstin Don Goldman's hitman?" Kit Sharper goes further.

"Is Uri Borstin a kingpin or a pawn?" Will contemplates aloud.

Chapter 63

Thursday, July 21, 2050.
An apartment building in Syracuse.

A custom-built FBI aeromobile quietly lands on a parking spot next to a brown apartment building in Syracuse, New York. The 50-year-old structure is clearly in dire need of renovation. Neighbors have been wondering about the health and safety of its tenants.

"Uri Borstin stayed in Unit 103 for three years, but I never saw him leave his apartment," the building super explains. "He ordered lots of food ... a lot for just one person. My personal opinion, anyway."

"Do you know where he moved to?" Agent Jones inquires.

"No idea. Sorry."

"Do you have a photo of him, by any chance?"

"We don't require our tenants to submit any photo."

"Who is the new tenant?" Agent Lee asks.

"Let me check our records ... David Neumann."

"May I speak to Mr. Neumann?"

"He must have left already. He goes out every day."

"Any idea where he goes?"

"Nope."

Chapter 64

Agent Jones steps into Kit Sharper's office with a box of bagels as Agent Lee trails him. He knows Kit shares his simple culinary taste for bagels with cream cheese.

"Where's the cheese?" asks Kit.

"Shit! Sorry, I forgot. But we have an update."

"OK, you're forgiven. Proceed."

"Uri Borstin lived in an apartment in Syracuse for three years—2044 to 2047. Never left his cave. Must be really overweight by now, judging from what the building super reports," Jones deadpans.

Kit Sharper tries to ignore the aside, but he winces at the unnecessary comment on Uri's weight, especially when he is just about to take a big bite of his bagel.

"The building manager doesn't know where Uri moved to," Jones adds.

"Or maybe ... the super is ... not telling us the truth." Kit wonders. "Do we know who's the new tenant?"

"A certain David Neumann. He left before we arrived."

"We need to talk to Mr. Willard again," adds Kit.

Chapter 65

Saturday, July 23, 2050.
Home of the Willards.

"Wish I could play golf again. Relaxes me," says Rich.

"Don't stress, Rich. Your wound needs to heal completely," Emily gently replies.

"You're right, honey," says Rich as he tries to slowly stretch his arms.

"Oh, I forgot to tell you. I got a call from the FBI yesterday afternoon. They want to talk again on Monday," says Rich.

Emily looks at him with concern.

"Everything will be fine," Rich assures his evidently worried wife.

Chapter 66

Monday, July 25, 2050.
FBI Cybercrime Unit Office.

Despite the fact that the optic of the day is Uri Borstin, Rich cannot get his mind to relax following a couple of sleepless nights. Money can buy a bed but not sleep, someone once said. And sleep deprivation can raise blood pressure and can result in an inability to focus.

The truth is that Rich is torn between being almost certain that Uri was the only one who called him "Rich-o" and having serious doubts that Uri would order his abduction. Certainly not for some minor verbal exchange with Uri at Columbia some thirty years ago.

"Uri was a quiet wiz. Topped all our exams in MBA. Rarely talked," Rich describes his former schoolmate to the agents gathered around the table.

"He dined alone most of the time. Didn't look at people in the eye. Read a lot. Ate a lot," adds Rich.

"Jones, please don't say overweight," Kit Sharper thinks to himself.

"So, Uri was overweight?" Agent Jones blurts out.

"Oh, come on, Jones, drop it, will ya!" Kit quips.

"Sorry, Kit. Anything else you remember, Mr. Willard?" asks Agent Jones.

"Oh, Uri at times interacted with one person. Equally brilliant. David Neumann," says Rich.

"David Neumann?"

"Yes."

"David Neumann is the current tenant of the apartment in Syracuse where Uri Borstin used to live," Agent Jones remarks, curiosity piqued.

"David lives in Syracuse?"

"That's what I just said."

"David dropped out on our second year in MBA. I heard that he assaulted someone and went to prison. School rumor ... nothing confirmed."

"Run a report on David Neumann," instructs Kit Sharper.

"Lee, get hold of Jason Ham. I want to see him in my office first thing tomorrow," Kit instructs.

Chapter 67

28 years ago. Monday, February 28, 2022.
Columbia University, Macroeconomics Class.

David Neumann and Uri Borstin sit at the back row of the classroom while Rich Willard and Bill Rivers sit right next to each other at the front row.

David Neumann is a graduate of Cornell University with a degree in Computer Engineering. He works for a global computer company as a Technical Specialist. With a promising upward career, he thinks that an MBA degree would be a good plus.

Uri Borstin holds a double degree in Computer Science and Electronics Engineering from MIT. Upon the prodding of his close friend, David Neumann, he decided to get an MBA before returning to MIT to obtain two doctoral degrees. Uri's insatiable appetite for knowledge stems from his strong personal belief that knowledge is power.

Rich Willard completed his Business Administration Honors program at Yale. He took an early interest in robotics while working for a midsize robotics company as a marketing and sales supervisor. Born into an affluent family, he has the resources to build a global business empire without the need to borrow a single Bit.

Bill Rivers holds a degree in Business Administration from Brown University. He comes from a family of wine connoisseurs and has set his eyes early in his career on building his own wine distribution company.

"Some 20 to 30 years from now, the world economic order will be much different from what we have today," their Professor, Charles Talbot, declares to his MBA class.

"Fast forward, robotics and AI will be the dominant forces that will drive labor into extinction," the Professor elaborates. "The coronavirus pandemic will be one of the catalysts that will push key industries to rethink the use of human laborers. It's a no-brainer. Machines do not get sick. They do not take vacations. Imagine a world where robots will take over most of the jobs: cooking, house cleaning, teaching, nursing, caring for the elderly or disabled, security, car assembly, airport porters, hotel concierge, warehousing, deliveries, and many more."

"That's it!" the young Rich Willard exclaims in his mind. "That's the business I will build ... robotics!" It's a moment of awakening that would mark the genesis of Willard Robotics.

"Economists estimate that around 60% of the world's population will be displaced. How will the jobless survive? Government dole outs," Professor Talbot goes on.

"The challenge is this: How do you tax robots? Sure, robots do not get tired, viruses can't knock them down, and they do not need Medicare and social security. But robots will not buy a house, take a vacation, dine in restaurants, shop for clothes—those human activities that will stir the global economy. So, what happens then?"

"All right, that's it for today, class," the Professor announces. "Submit your reaction paper on this topic by Friday, 3PM. Class dismissed."

Everyone leaves the classroom except Uri Borstin, who seems to be deep in thought.

Just before Rich steps out of the room, he realizes that he left his mobile phone on his seat. He goes back and sees Uri.

"Hey, Uri. Don't be lazy. Move your butt. It's time for our next class, you bum," Rich needles him in his usual cocky voice, unaware that Uri is enraged by his rude manners. And after a dozen encounters, Uri has had enough.

"That's it, Rich-o! Stop pushing people around," Uri shoots back in a rare demonstration of anger.

"Did you just call me Rich-o, you shithead?" Rich takes offense.

"You heard me, moron!"

"That's it! Go back to your home country! We don't need you here, you slimy pig!"

"I was born here, idiot," quips Uri.

Rich was stunned by Uri's curveball.

Realizing that he just started a battle he cannot win, Rich retreats and says, "Forget what I said. I didn't mean it."

"I'm sure you did, stupid!" Uri quips.

Chapter 68

Monday, July 25, 2050, 8:00PM.
Home of the Willards.

Rich and Emily move from the dining area to the living room as a house robot clears away the dirty dishes and places them in the dishwasher.

Emily orders the robot to prepare two cups of tea after cleaning the dining table.

As they sit on their 20,000-Bit couch, Emily updates Rich on Margie's progress with a therapist.

"Maybe I should see a therapist myself," Rich muses.

Emily looks at Rich and gently nods.

"Honey, do you remember Uri Borstin?" Rich asks his wife.

"Your classmate in Columbia?"

"Yes, that's him. He got two PhDs. One in Artificial Intelligence and another in Cryptography," Rich murmurs absently.

"Are you thinking of hiring him?"

"No." Rich's mind is elsewhere.

"What's with him?" Emily brings him back.

"Chief Architect of Dreamscape, but seemingly disappeared into thin air."

"Oh, really? That's sad news."

"Yeah."

"Does that mean our investment in Dreamscape will crash?" Emily curiously asks.

"Don't worry. Won't break our bank."

Chapter 69

Agent Jason Ham sits opposite Kit Sharper.

Kit offers him coffee. Jason declines.

"Coffee isn't good for my hyperactive brain," explains Agent Ham.

His expensive coat and barbered appearance hide the fact that he used to be Public Enemy Number One for breaching the systems of the FBI, CIA, and NSA when he was a teenager ... not too long ago. The FBI quickly recruited him to keep a better eye on him.

In his early twenties, Jason Ham is a rookie by agency definition, though, unknown to many, he is an esteemed master among the top hackers in the world.

"Thank you for coming at short notice, Agent Ham. We need your expertise," Kit reveals.

"How can I help?"

Chapter 70

Wednesday, July 27, 2050.
Office of Agent Jason Ham.

Agent Ham's office is unmistakably a geeky camp where any young egghead would want to pitch a tent.

Sophisticated electronic surveillance gadgets that are not available to the public, ultra-modern monitors that follow voice commands or a simple wave of a hand, and most important of all, top secret clearance to use the fastest cluster of quantum supercomputers that can access any data from anywhere in the world, including those that are captured by thousands of satellites constantly scanning the planet.

Ham murmurs to himself as he gazes intently at his monitors.

"Wow, this Uri Borstin is good. No online footprint. Not even a bank account registered to his name," he tells himself. "I wonder how he gets his salary."

"Time to call Kit."

"Hello, Kit. Not much information on Uri Borstin in the global network. Can you please arrange for me to talk to the head of their Systems & Network Operations?"

"Why?"

"I have a few ideas to explore."

"Lee and Jones paid their Tech Lead a visit last week. I'll ask them to reach out to him and go with you. Just don't mention Uri Borstin. We don't want them to think we're investigating him. Borstin reports directly to the CEO."

"Got it."

Chapter 71

Thursday, July 28, 2050.
Dreamscape Head Office.

"Roger, thanks for accommodating us at such short notice. This is Jason Ham, my colleague at the Bureau," says Agent Jones as he introduces Jason to Roger DeKalb, Dreamscape Tech Lead.

"You've met Agent Lee," Agent Jones tilts his head towards Jenny.

"Agent Ham has a few questions," Jones adds.

"How can I help?" asks Roger.

"Thank you for seeing us."

"No worries."

"Dreamscape runs on your proprietary platform, correct?"

"Yes. That's public knowledge."

"How big is your software development team?"

"I don't know the exact number, but it is a small team."

"Who leads that team?"

"Our Chief Architect, Uri Borstin. I gave this information to Agent Jones a few days ago. Are you investigating Uri?"

"We're just gathering information."

"I am not saying anything new. Uri wrote a big portion of the main operating system of Dreamscape."

"Do you know if his team members have access to Uri's code?"

"No one is allowed to access Uri's work. Ordered by our president, Don Goldman. Company confidential."

"How does Uri test his code?"

"I don't know. I don't know of anyone who did software testing with Uri. I mean, the whole Dreamscape technology, including the use of our microchip. It is our company's intellectual property. Confidential."

"No one in your company knows what Uri does?"

"Why are you interested in what Uri does? Did he do anything wrong?"

"I didn't say that."

"It is common practice for tech companies to closely guard their intellectual property. No one in our company is authorized to view Uri's work. Uri reports to Don Goldman, so Don must know. However, Don is not technical. He manages the company's financials."

"Right. But what if Uri is run over by a truck tomorrow?"

"I don't know the answer to that. I'm sure Don has a Plan B."

"OK. On another topic, do you have a network operations team that can monitor the flow of data?" Ham shifts direction.

"Yes. Why?"

"I just want to see if there are unusual packets of data."

"Not really sure what you mean by 'unusual packets of data.' Besides, we have an extremely large amount of data."

"Got it. Just want to talk to your network ops team."

"OK, I will connect you with them," Roger nods.

"Thank you," Ham nods in return.

As soon as the agents leave, Roger calls Don Goldman and reports the conversation.

"Do I need to be worried?" asks Don Goldman.

"I don't think they will find anything," Roger assures him.

Chapter 72

Jason Ham enters a large hall that resembles a command center for launching spacecraft and satellites.

One can't miss the gigantic wall-to-wall, floor-to-ceiling screen that shows a map of the world with a multitude of colored dots spanning nearly the entire globe. Each dot represents a Dreamscape user.

"Red represents an active session. Yellow is inactive," explains Siva Raja, the tech lead.

"Can you trace data packets?" asks Jason.

"We have the most advanced packet tracing technology available in the market," Siva says proudly.

"Good. So, let me tell you what I'm looking for," says Agent Ham.

"I am looking for any unusual packets moving in Dreamscape," he specifies.

"That's very vague. Give me an example," says Siva.

"Unusual volume of data traffic or connections."

"Hmmm ... go ahead. I'm taking notes."

"OK. Also, packets that are encrypted," Jason goes on.

"Agent Ham, all our data is encrypted," explains Siva.

"And you have the keys to decrypt them, right?"

"Yes, but we don't decrypt subscriber data. We protect privacy."

"Hmmm ... anyway, let's just look for encrypted data that you cannot decrypt."

"I don't think you heard me."

"I did."

"Well, I am not sure that what you're looking for even exists in Dreamscape," Siva retorts sarcastically.

"Just humor me, Siva," Agent Ham replies with a smile.

Chapter 73

Kit Sharper appears as a hologram to FBI Director, Will Bridges.

"Will, no one in Dreamscape can access Uri Borstin's code. His work is considered 'Company Confidential.' They don't even know how Uri tests his software code."

"Lived in Syracuse for three years, but no longer there," Kit adds.

"His present location?"

"We're still checking."

"So, what's our plan?"

"We got Agent Ham exploring some possible leads. He's working with the Dreamscape network operations team."

"We sure Borstin is the one who abducted Rich Willard?"

"Not 100%. We only have the word of Willard that Uri is the only one who called him Rich-o."

"That's lame. Besides, what could be Borstin's motive?"

"We don't know yet."

"I'm not convinced. We might be wasting our time on the wrong person, Kit."

Chapter 74

Wednesday, August 3, 2050.
Dreamscape Global Command Center.

"Hello, Kit. Just an update. Been here in Dreamscape Command Center since Monday and we haven't found anything yet," reports Agent Jason Ham to Cybercrime Unit Head, Kit Sharper.

"That's disappointing," Kit says, putting his coffee mug down.

"Well, give me a couple more days," Jason adds.

"OK. Keep me posted," directs Kit.

"Will do."

As Agent Ham opens the door to the Command Center, Siva Raja raises his hand to call Jason's attention.

"I found something," Siva announces.

"What?"

"I've been observing an intermittent burst of data coming from one location in New York to many different places across the globe."

"Is that unusual?" asks Jason.

"Not exactly. However, remember I told you that our all our data is encrypted?" Siva points out. "Well, I know we are bound by privacy agreements with our subscribers, but I just tried to quickly decrypt a short string of data coming from this location and ... none of our encryption keys work."

"And it's connecting to ports that are not registered in our database," Siva sounds intrigued.

"Can you tell me that exact location where the data is coming from and where it is going?" asks Ham.

Chapter 75

Wednesday, August 3, 2050.
FBI office.

Kit Sharper sits quietly in front of a handful of agents as he ponders the information that his team currently holds.

His thumb gently rubs his coffee mug's ear while his eyes stare at a far corner of his office.

"We're not making much progress ... patience ... patience," he thinks to himself. As Kit has been through roads like this before, he knows very well that perseverance is the key. It's a marathon. Those who endure will eventually get to the finish line.

Kit turns to his team. "What do we have on David Neumann?"

"He lives in an apartment building in Syracuse previously owned by Uri Borstin. David regularly visits an apartment in Ithaca, about fifty miles away." Jones replies.

"Do we know who he visits in Ithaca?"

"The registered tenant is an old lady by the name of Glenda Terrain."

"Get to it then."

Chapter 76

Wednesday, August 3, 2050.
Dreamscape Global Command Center.

"Can you run a trace to determine the exact location where the encrypted packets are going?" asks Jason.

After a few minutes studying his monitor, Siva's eyes widen in amazement.

"Oh, interesting. These bursts of data ... they're like hundreds of AI bots across the globe working together ... like they have their own internal network within Dreamscape."

"Great! Can you give me a list of those locations?" asks Agent Ham.

"Not easy."

"How much time do you need?"

"Give me a day."

"OK," Agent Ham gives a thumbs up as he steps out to call Kit Sharper.

Chapter 77

Friday, August 5, 2050.
FBI office.

It's Friday. And it's summer. The bright and sunny day is enough reason for people to go out and enjoy the parks. Kit Sharper looks through his office window and wonders when he last had a chance to enjoy a relaxing stroll with his family.

His reflections are rudely interrupted by a familiar beep. He turns around and Agent Jones appears as a hologram in front of him.

"Glenda Terrain was born and raised in Ithaca, New York. Never married. She is an aunt of David Neumann and the only sibling of David's mom. Maybe his only living relative," reports Agent Jones.

"OK. That makes sense that he visits her every day. What else do we know?"

"We also got some info from old Internet archives. Old photos of Glenda Terrain and her best friend, Tasha Borstin, in front of Glenda's restaurant."

"Is her restaurant still operating?"

"No, it was sold seven years ago when she retired."

"Run a report on Tasha Borstin."

Chapter 78

Friday, August 5, 2050.
Dreamscape Global Command Center.

"Here's the list of addresses that you requested," Siva Raja shows Agent Jason the information on his large transparent monitor.

"I've grouped the sources and destinations of this specially encrypted data ... 52 locations."

"Any of those 52 located in the US?" asks Agent Ham.

"Yes, two locations. One in New Jersey and another one in Ithaca, New York," Siva replies.

"What's the address in Ithaca?" Agent Ham leans forward.

"1205 Base Line Road, Ithaca, New York."

Chapter 79

Friday, August 5, 2050.
FBI office.

Jones appears as a hologram in front of Kit Sharper.

"Sir, I have an update on Tasha Borstin."

"Go."

"Tasha Borstin came to the US in 1988, overstayed, and became an illegal. Glenda Terrain petitioned Tasha Borstin to work in her restaurant in Ithaca, New York. In three of Glenda's posts in the old Internet, she refers to Tasha as her best friend."

"Is Tasha still alive?"

"Tasha passed away five years ago. February 12, 2045."

"Does Tasha have a family?"

"She traveled to the US as a single person. According to hospital records, she bore two sons, three years apart. Her firstborn son is Uri Borstin."

"Excellent! And the second son?"

"Dmitri Borstin. Also known as Dima. Apparently, she left Dmitri in the hospital. The hospital arranged for adoption."

"What is the name of Tasha's husband?"

"No marriage certificates. The birth certificates of her two sons showed Howard Kirby as the father. Howard Kirby has no record of employment."

"Interesting. OK. Let's have a team meeting. You, Lee, Yoder, and Ham on Monday here in my office," the cyber head taps his desk.

Chapter 80

Monday, August 8, 2050.
Kit Sharper's FBI Office.

"Bagels and coffee," Kit Sharper offers his team members. "Grab one and pass."

"Someone forgot to buy cream cheese again," protests Agent Lee.

"Guilty," Agent Jones kiddingly quips.

"That's it. I'm leaving," Lee says jokingly.

"Team, let's analyze the data that we have so far," Kit cuts in.

"Let's start with you, Ham," he adds.

Agent Jason Ham looks at his notes and reports, "We spotted an anomaly in Dreamscape. Specially encrypted data is being exchanged with 52 locations across the globe. We have two locations here in the US: one in New Jersey and another one in New York."

"Specially encrypted data… what do you mean?" Kit Sharper asks.

"None of their registered encryption keys work," says Agent Ham.

"Doesn't make sense. How can that happen?"

"Someone is using a set of encryption keys unknown to Dreamscape's technical specialists," the agent explains.

"How?"

"Must be installed and maintained by another team."

"Uri Borstin?"

"Don't know."

"Interesting," Agent Jones butts in "Let's go back to your list of 52 locations. You mentioned New York. Where in New York?"

"1205 Base Line Road in Ithaca," Agent Ham replies.

"That's where David Neumann's aunt lives," Jones exclaims as he re-checks his notes.

"How about the address in New Jersey?" Kit Sharper adds.

Agent Ham pauses for some momentary suspense.

"C'mon, Ham, say it," Kit nudges.

"It's 1304 Clover Drive, Elizabeth, New Jersey," says Agent Ham.

"Hey, isn't that the address of the warehouse in New Jersey where Margie Willard was held?" asks Lee.

Chapter 81

Monday, August 8, 2050.
1205 Base Line Road in Ithaca.

"I will take care of you, Aunt Glenda. A promise is a promise," David Neumann says to himself as his 10-year-old driverless car parks in front of 1205 Base Line Road, Ithaca, New York.

David is a gentle giant of 270 pounds in a six-foot-four-inch frame. A very shy and private person, he usually walks with his head down to avoid eye contact with anyone. With an IQ of a genius, he has a voracious appetite for knowledge and trivia. His abundant spare time is mostly spent building model planes and watching Kung Fu films. David trained himself on martial arts, though he will never brag about it. Arrogance is not in his nature.

David was finishing his MBA at Columbia University when his life was harshly interrupted.

He intervened in a fight between a rowdy customer and a waitress, Tasha Borstin, in his Aunt Glenda's restaurant that resulted in the customer getting severely concussed. David gave the salacious diner a Kung Fu chop that instantly knocked the braggart to the ground. David was convicted and spent time in prison.

His Aunt Glenda and her best friend, Tasha Borstin, never failed to visit him during his years of incarceration.

Realizing that David's future was ruined, Glenda wrote in her will that, if anything were to happen to her, her nephew would inherit everything she owned. When Glenda gave a copy of her Last Will and Testament to David, he promised her that, in the event that she could no longer take care of herself, he would look after her.

David opens the front door of 1205 Base Line Road with his fingerprint.

He calls out, "Hi, Aunt Glenda, I'm here. Time for your regular check-up."

A humanoid robot greets him.

Chapter 82

Monday, August 8, 2050.
Kit Sharper's FBI Office.

Kit Sharper's excitement over the progress in the Dreamscape investigation is palpable.

Kit grew up putting together 1,000-piece puzzles and solving riddles that would usually bore other people. Unconsciously, he had been training himself to connect dots—hundreds of dots and pieces of information to form a picture or a story. Those were the kinds of things that would perk him up even as far back as his growing up years in Brooklyn. Kit was a straight A student from elementary to college. It wasn't a surprise to many when he got a full scholarship to New York University and graduated with honors upon completion of a double degree in computer engineering and finance.

He holds numerous certificates on cyber security backed by decades of experience as Chief Information Security Officer in top government agencies. His talent for solving complex problems is what led him to his current role as Chief of the FBI Cybercrime Unit.

Kit is also widely known as the agent who tracked down Jason Ham, a Boston tech wizard, when the latter hacked several key government systems. Spotting Jason's extraordinary skills, the cyber chief persuaded the agency that Jason would be a great asset.

"Any other location in the US?" Kit Sharper probes.

Agent Ham looks at his list, "No."

"OK. Find a way to talk to David Neumann," Kit is emphatic as he addresses Lee, Jones, Yoder, and Ham.

"We also need more information on Glenda Terrain. We know she's retired, but let's find out what she does. And any information David can give us about Uri Borstin."

Chapter 83

Monday, August 8, 2050.
1205 Base Line Road in Ithaca.

Glenda Terrain's house is a 3,000-square-foot ranch-style bungalow. She bought it 20 years ago with her savings from her restaurant business. A self-made college dropout, she devoted most of her adult life building her dream restaurant, painting, listening to classical music, and helping her good friend, Tasha Borstin.

It is no wonder that her oil paintings of landscapes and flowers dominate the walls of her house. Bright-colored sunflowers. She signs her oil paintings with her initials, "GT." Glenda is all about simplicity.

"Hi, Aunt Glenda. I brought you sunflowers. Your favorite. I dropped by a grocery store on my way and got me an egg sandwich. You used to prepare egg sandwiches for Mom and me for breakfast when I was a kid, remember? I still love them to this day," David smiles as he arranges the sunflowers in a vase.

There is no response to his greeting other than a whirring sound and some random beeps from a robot moving around Glenda's bed.

Chapter 84

Monday, August 8, 2050.
Kit Sharper's FBI Office.

"Any location in France?" Kit Sharper asks in his thick Brooklyn accent as he writes down some notes.

"Yes, one. 62 Rue de Marivaux, Montreuil," Agent Ham replies.

"Montreuil ... that sounds familiar," the chief muses with a faraway look as though searching for some answers from empty space.

"Hmm ... Director Bridges gave me a copy of the report from the French Intelligence Agency ... it's here somewhere ... got it."

"OK. What was that address again, Jason?" Kit asks.

"62 Rue de Marivaux, Montreuil."

"Ha! We have a match," Kit exclaims.

Chapter 85

Wednesday, August 10, 2050.
1205 Base Line Road in Ithaca.

Jones, Lee, and Ham cross the street as David Neumann's flying car lands in front of 1205 Base Line Road in Ithaca.

"Are you David Neumann?" asks Ham as David steps out of his car and closes the door.

"No," David answers curtly as he tries to walk back to his car, avoiding eye contact.

"We know who you are, Neumann," says Jones, putting his hand on the door.

"I am not him, so go away," exclaims David.

"You are David Neumann," insists Agent Lee.

"No, I am not. Who are you anyway?"

"I am Agent Lee. This is Agent Jones. That's Agent Ham. We are from the FBI."

"I have done nothing wrong!" David shouts. "Go away! You're harassing me!"

"Calm down, David. We are not harassing you. We just need to ask a few questions," Ham tries to pacify him.

After what seems like eternity, David raises his head, stares blankly at a nearby house, and says, "What questions?"

"Can we go inside the house and talk there?"

"No. We can talk here," David mutters as he leads the Feds away from Glenda's property.

Chapter 86

FBI Director Will Bridges appears as a hologram in front of Kit Sharper.

"Kit, we just received another update from the French."

"Do you remember the warehouse near Paris where Willard was held hostage?"

"What about it?"

"Remember they found crates of bottled water in that warehouse?" Bridges reminds.

Kit Sharper stares at his boss for a few moments while trying to dig into his memory chest. Something clicks. "Warehouse is operated by Rainwater ... Bottled water donated to Africa, the Middle East, and Asia ... Wait. What do you mean?"

"It appears there is more to it."

"I'm listening."

Chapter 87

Wednesday, August 10, 2050.
1205 Base Line Road in Ithaca.

"Do you know Uri Borstin?" asks Agent Jones.

"He is the son of my aunt's best friend."

"How long have you known Uri?"

"We went to the same high school here in Ithaca. Then the same university for our MBA."

"Columbia?" asks Agent Lee.

David nods. "How did you know?"

"Where is Uri now?" Agent Lee inquires.

"I don't know."

"What is the name of Uri's mother?" asks Agent Ham, verifying if David's response will match the information that they have.

"Tasha. Tasha Borstin. She worked in the restaurant of my aunt. Tasha died five years ago."

"Does Uri have any siblings?" the agent goes on.

"He has one brother. Born Dmitri Borstin. He was adopted and named Robert."

"Last name?" asks Agent Ham.

"Devall. Robert Devall."

"Robert Devall ... hmm ... sounds familiar," Jones tells himself.

"Know where he lives?" The questions are coming in quick succession.

"No."

"What's the name of your aunt?" asks Agent Lee.

"Glenda. Glenda Terrain."

"Where does Glenda live?"

Chapter 88

Wednesday, August 10, 2050.
Kit Sharper's FBI Office.

"The French ran some tests on the Rainwater bottled water. They found it contaminated with a compound that attacks the central nervous system ... over time. Starts with tingling in your feet that progresses all the way to your lungs.

"When it gets to the chest area," Will Bridges adds, "people die from difficulty in breathing."

"There's was some news months ago about people in Africa, Asia, and the Middle East ... dying of some respiratory illness," Kit recalls.

"Right. The French report might provide the missing link."

"What's the name of the compound?" Sharper asks.

"It's in the report. I just sent it to you," Bridges answers.

"Thanks. I'll also ask Yoder to read it. Might as well use his master's degree in Chemistry," Sharper replies.

"Ok."

"Something's very wrong with these people," Kit shakes his head.

"So, what is Rich Willard's connection with Rainwater? Why would they abduct him?" Kit ponders. "We need to talk to Willard again."

Chapter 89

Wednesday, August 10, 2050.
1205 Base Line Road in Ithaca.

"She lives there," David Neumann says to Agents Jones, Ham, and Lee as he points to Glenda's home.

"She lives alone?" asks Agent Lee.

"Yes."

"Can we talk to her?"

"Not possible," says David.

"Why?" asks Agent Jones.

"She is asleep."

"Oh ... we can come back tomorrow," Agent Jones comments.

"Wait. May we just look inside the house even for a minute?" Agent Lee requests in a calm tone.

"One minute," David nods. "You'll see what I mean."

"Thanks," Lee says quietly.

Chapter 90

Wednesday, August 10, 2050.
Will Bridges' FBI Office.

"Any update on Dreamscape?" asks Will Bridges as a hologram of Kit Sharper appears.

"Ham found encrypted data traffic within Dreamscape that cannot be decrypted by any of their keys."

"Translate," Bridges barks.

"Someone in their company is using Dreamscape as a means to send and receive specially encrypted data."

"Is that a problem?"

"It is. That means that the data cannot be read by anyone else in Dreamscape."

"And?"

"They found many locations around the world that send and receive this specially encrypted data. At least two locations connected with Rainwater."

"What two locations?"

"One is the warehouse outside Paris where Rich Willard was abducted; the other is a warehouse in New Jersey where his daughter was held when she was kidnapped."

Chapter 91

Wednesday, August 10, 2050.
1205 Base Line Road in Ithaca.

The overpowering odor of a strong antiseptic mixed with some medicated oil hits the agents as soon as they enter the room.

A humanoid meets them and recognizes David.

"They're friends," says David as he waves his hand as though giving instructions to the humanoid not to harm them.

"You have visitors, Aunt Glenda," David calls out. Silence meets David's greetings.

The FBI agents see a very old woman lying on a hospital bed. A respirator whirs next to the bed.

They notice the feeding tube running out of her mouth. The sight and the smell seem to make Ham a little queasy but a quick stare from Jones is enough to hold him together. Lee looks at them with a tinge of embarrassment.

David gently shifts his aunt onto her left side to check for rashes and bed sores.

Ham notices a chip behind Glenda's ear.

"Looks like a NeuNet chip," Agent Ham makes a mental note as he also observes Lee's attention to details.

David carefully moves Glenda back. When he pulls the blanket to cover his aunt, Lee notices what appear to be some random lines tattooed on her left arm.

She quickly takes photos of the tattoos while David briefly leaves the room.

Chapter 92

Friday, August 12, 2050, 10:00AM.
Kit Sharper's FBI Office.

"Thanks for meeting with us," Kit Sharper to Rich Willard.

"We just have a few questions," Agent Lee adds.

Willard nods.

"You mentioned in our first meeting that you sent three million Bits to Juliette LeMont because you were exploring a business opportunity with her."

"What is that business?" the agent asks.

Rich just stares at the two government officers. They wait patiently.

"It was an error in judgement," Rich suddenly blurts out.

"I was not exploring any business with Ms. LeMont. I was blackmailed."

There was a long pause in the room.

The silence was broken by Kit.

"Please continue."

"Dreamscape, for me, was an escape from the pressures of my work. I met Juliette LeMont and ... she was ... accommodating," Rich begins.

"One thing led to another and after meeting Ms. LeMont in Paris, I received a package with photos of us and a demand for three million Bits."

"I was threatened ... if I didn't pay ... it could destroy everything I worked for ... and hurt my family," Rich admits.

Chapter 93

Friday, August 12, 2050, 10:00AM Eastern Time.
1205 Base Line Road in Ithaca.

David Neumann arrives at Glenda's house.

He has a bouquet of fresh sunflowers, his aunt's favorite.

He opens the door and says, "Hi, Aunt Glenda, I'm here."

He removes the wilted sunflowers from a vase and replaces them with fresh ones.

After checking his aunt's vital signs, David makes a call.

"Hi, Dr. Kiev. See you in 15 minutes?"

Chapter 94

Friday, August 12, 2050.
Kit Sharper's FBI Office.

"I wish you had been honest with us the first time," Kit says with a stern look.

Rich sighs. "Sorry."

"We have been suspecting that Ms. LeMont works for a syndicate that victimizes the rich."

"Then we received new info that she is somehow connected with a charity organization called Rainwater," Agent Lee reveals.

"Charity?"

"Yes."

"The warehouse outside Paris where you were taken is rented by Rainwater," Kit Sharper puts in. "The warehouse in New Jersey where they took your daughter is also leased by Rainwater."

"Doesn't make sense. A charity organization that blackmails and kidnaps people?" asks Rich with a puzzled look on his face.

Chapter 95

Friday, August 12, 2050.
1205 Base Line Road in Ithaca.

A grey autonomous car parks in front of Glenda's house.

Dr. Ana Kiev, a retired physician, puts on a surgical mask and steps out of her car carrying a bag of medical supplies.

David opens the door and greets her, "Nice to see you again, Dr. Kiev. Come in."

A humanoid robot approaches the visitor and says, "Welcome back, Dr. Kiev."

Ana checks on Glenda's vital signs.

"She's doing fine. Nothing to worry about. But you have to get someone to regularly wash her," the doctor points out.

"The nursing aide has been sick for two weeks," explains David as he prepares a cup of breakfast tea for Dr. Kiev.

Then, he asks, "When will she come out of her coma, Doctor?"

"Sorry, David. I don't know. She may not come out of it," Dr. Kiev patiently answers. He asks her the same question every time they meet.

David sighs. "I understand ... Please ... have some tea."

"Thanks, David."

"Good thing, we have Dreamscape," David ponders.

Chapter 96

Friday, August 12, 2050.
Kit Sharper's FBI Office.

"Seems to be a rather odd combination, a charity organization blackmailing folks," Agent Jenny Lee wonders aloud.

"Rainwater's operation is completely automated using robotics and AI. They may even be using your robots, Mr. Willard. Not sure how they can afford it, though."

"We give heavy discounts to charity organizations. Like 90% or more," says Rich.

"Did you deal directly with Rainwater?" asks Agent Lee.

"I have hundreds of thousands of customers around the world. I have sales people for that," replies Rich.

"With 20,000 people donating a few Bits a month, it isn't possible to sustain Rainwater's level of operations," Lee points out.

"I do recall ... Rainwater approached me ... a few years ago ... for donations."

"And?"

"I declined! Charity? Any charity is lame! I have no patience for weak and lazy people," explains Rich as he defaults back to his usual cocky way.

The agents exchange looks of disbelief, surprised by such an arrogant comment from the billionaire.

"That's so insensitive for you to say," Agent Lee is unable to hide her disgust.

"You mean I should be thankful for the homeless and unemployed? Listen. I have over 50,000 people in my payroll. We all work. Every one of us. So, now I owe money to those who don't work?" Rich quips sarcastically.

Kit Sharper can tell his rookies are about to breathe fire through their nostrils. He quickly shifts gears.

"Rainwater operates a small desalination plant ... and a water bottling facility ... Fully automated," Kit narrates.

"Well ... I am sure they get heavy discounts on equipment and supplies, too," says Rich. "I tell you, these charity organizations ... they are scams! Don't you get it?"

"We hear you, Mr. Willard. Rainwater gets all these discounts. But do you know what they really do?" Agent Lee voices what everyone is thinking.

Chapter 97

Friday, August 12, 2050.
1205 Base Line Road in Ithaca.

David opens a door that leads to the basement of Glenda's house.

"Watch your steps, Dr. Kiev. We don't want another freak accident," says David as they walk down the stairs leading to the basement.

The room is an ultramodern intensive care operating theater outfitted with medical equipment that any premier hospital would have.

Two humanoid robots greet them.

Chapter 98

"Rainwater distributes bottled water to three continents—Africa, Asia, and the Middle East," Sharper intones.

"For free," he adds.

"I bet it's a scam," says Rich.

"Not quite," Lee interjects.

"The French found crates of bottled water in the warehouse where you were abducted," Kit explains. "They ran tests and determined that the water in those bottles is contaminated by a compound that is commonly found in water that we drink. Small amounts won't hurt. However, slightly increased levels cause neurologic disorders. Hard to detect."

"In other words, they are slowly killing people. Millions of people. Perhaps billions."

"Shit!" exclaims Rich as his jaw drops in disbelief.

Agents Lee, Jones, Yoder, and Ham look at each other with palpable excitement as their investigation is now taking shape.

"And Juliette LeMont works for Rainwater ... that poisons people?" asks Rich in alarm.

"Their modus operandi is quite simple. LeMont sets up a rendezvous. She kisses the unsuspecting victim in public while someone takes photos, which will then be used to extort money."

"But you told me before that none goes to Juliette's bank account. Where does the money go?"

"We traced the three million Bits that you remitted. Hopped through four accounts and landed on an account owned by Robert Devall, CEO of Rainwater," explains Kit Sharper.

"Fuck!" Rich quips.

"There's another thing that will interest you," says Agent Lee.

Chapter 99

Friday, August 12, 2050.
1205 Base Line Road in Ithaca.

"Vital signs are good," Dr. Kiev announces.

"I haven't been getting any medical alerts from the robots for some months now, so everything seems to be on the up and up," she adds.

"Please bill me for your services, Dr. Kiev," David reminds her.

"Don't worry about it. Tasha and I were friends since we were in our teens. She was the one who convinced me to fly with her to the US back in 1988. To find a new life here. So sad to see her go."

"This is my way of giving back to Tasha. And to Glenda, for helping my friend."

Chapter 100

"Robert Devall ... the CEO of Rainwater ... is the brother ... of your classmate." Kit Sharper explains.

"Who?"

"Remember Uri Borstin?" Agent Lee asks.

"Yes?" Willard looks up in complete shock and blurts, "Oh shit! Don't tell me!"

"Yes, Uri Borstin is the brother of Robert Devall."

"How?"

"Robert was born Dmitri Borstin. Was adopted and became Robert Devall."

"You mean, the Devall family of the bottled water empire?"

"Exactly."

"The Devall family is super rich. They don't need to extort money from anyone to do their charity work."

"True. But when the Devall patriarch died, his two sons did some legal maneuvering that left Robert with almost nothing."

"Fuck! So, the rumors were true!" Rich tells himself.

"So, Robert decided to set up Rainwater...his own water bottling ... charity work ... on the surface." Lee explains.

"And although Robert is the CEO, we believe he works for someone else," adds Lee.

"Who?"

"Your classmate, Uri."

"Uri is the Chief Architect of Dreamscape. What has he got to do with Rainwater?"

"We suspect that Uri is using Dreamscape to control Rainwater operations without being monitored by WorldGov authorities."

"Dreamscape is protected by laws," Kit Sharper adds. "They are not subject to WorldGov surveillance."

"Rainwater receives donations from public donors ... but not enough to sustain its global operations."

"So, they resort to extortion?" asks Rich.

"Yup," Lee nods.

"I get it. But I don't understand why Uri would want to kill people using contaminated water."

"That we don't know yet," Kit admits.

"Anyway, my techies in Willard Robotics can stop him," Rich assures.

"Not exactly," Agent Ham interjects. "Uri uses encryption keys that he alone knows. His communication with all Rainwater facilities cannot be decrypted by anyone in Dreamscape."

Rich nods slowly, "I am not surprised. The guy is a super genius."

"The big question is this: Is Uri taking orders from Goldman or has he gone rogue?" asks Sharper.

Chapter 101

Friday, August 12, 2050.
1205 Base Line Road in Ithaca.

"Have you heard from Dima lately?" Dr. Kiev asks David.

"You mean Robert."

"Well, he will always be Dima to me," smiles the doctor.

"The last time I saw him was over five years ago when he and Uri reconnected, months before Tasha passed away," David recounts.

"Tasha's life was something else," Dr. Kiev reminisces. "She meets this bum, Howard Kirby, in Glenda's restaurant. She gives birth to Uri and Dmitri. Decides to raise Uri and gives Dmitri up for adoption."

"I know. And then the bastard beats Uri every single day," says David, shaking his head in disbelief.

"Dmitri was adopted by the Devalls ... of that bottled water empire," the doctor recalls. "His adoptive father, Frank Devall, treated him like his own son and taught him the water bottling business.

"However, just before Frank died, Dmitri's siblings manipulated Frank's Last Will and Testament that left Dmitri with just a few thousand Bits."

She adds sadly, "Tasha, before she passed away, told me that Dima was very bitter ... resented being given away for adoption ... hated his Devall siblings. She said that Dima completely lost faith in humanity. He wanted to find his own place under the sun. He found it in Europe."

"I'm glad that you helped Uri and Dmitri reconnect before Tasha passed away," Dr. Kiev turns to David with a smile.

"I just do what I can."

Chapter 102

Monday, August 15, 2050, 10:20AM.
Kit Sharper's FBI Office.

Kit Sharper looks out his office window as Agents Lee, Jones, Yoder, and Ham enter the room.

"We still have no clue as to Uri Borstin's whereabouts," Sharper begins as he takes a seat.

"Even David Neumann has no clue where Uri is," says Jones.

"We saw his Aunt Glenda who is comatose," says Ham with Lee and Jones nodding in agreement.

"Coma? Something doesn't square here. Isn't Ithaca one of the locations in the list provided by Dreamscape?" asks Sharper.

"Yes."

"So, if Glenda's house is part of Rainwater operations, how does a person in a coma fit into the puzzle?" Kit wonders aloud.

"Then David Neumann must be part of Rainwater," Kit adds.

"Hmmm ... not sure about that," Lee interjects.

"I noticed that Glenda has a chip behind her ear," adds Lee.

No one seems to catch what Agent Lee is hinting at.

After a short pause, they forge ahead.

"What is her connection to Rainwater ... any ideas?" the cyber chief asks.

"Let me get back to you on that. I need to touch base again with Roger DeKalb," says Ham.

"OK. Anything else that you found unusual?" Kit pushes.

"Glenda has some random lines ... sort of like bar codes ... on her left arm," says Lee.

"What's unusual about that?" asks Kit.

"Why would anyone tattoo barcodes on their arm?" argues Jones.

Kit pauses for a moment. He remembers some of his own friends who came up with out-of-this world designs for their tattoos.

"OK. Let's take note of that. Still leaves us with the question: Where the hell is Borstin?"

Chapter 103

Wednesday, August 17, 2050.
Dreamscape Office.

"Hi, Roger. You've met my colleagues, Agent Jones and Agent Lee, before," says Ham to Roger DeKalb, Dreamscape Technical Lead.

"I have. So, how can I help you?" asks Roger.

"Siva gave us a list of locations where some specially encrypted data is being transmitted and received. We need more detailed information," says Agent Ham.

"What sort of detailed information?" Roger sounds cautious.

"We need the type and number of devices in those locations," Agent Ham presses on.

"What do you mean by 'type'?"

"I mean like Dreamscape microchip, printer, robots, drones, CCTV cameras, and so on," the agent explains.

"I think we can do that," Roger agrees. "Let me call Siva."

"How long do you think it will take to produce that list?" asks Agent Jones.

"Give us a day or two," the tech lead replies.

As soon as the Feds leave, Roger calls Don Goldman.

"They are looking for more details on the locations that we gave them," Roger reports. Don stares ahead, worried.

Chapter 104

Thursday, August 18, 2050.
1205 Base Line Road in Ithaca.

David Neumann's flying car parks itself in front of Glenda Terrain's house.

As David steps out of his car, the nursing aide approaches him.

"Hi, Ms. Lubbock," he greets her. "I'm glad you're OK."

"Just some bad flu, but I feel much better now," the caregiver explains, adjusting her mask.

They walk towards the house together.

Chapter 105

Thursday, August 18, 2050.
Dreamscape Office.

"Kit, we got the list from Dreamscape," reports Ham to FBI Cybercrime Unit Head, Kit Sharper.

"And?"

"Glenda's house in Ithaca is a data center."

"What do you mean? I thought you, Jones, and Lee didn't find anything in Glenda's house?" asks Kit.

"That's right. But this new information indicates that there are hundreds of servers in that location," Ham stresses.

"Didn't you all tell me that Glenda Terrain is in coma?"

"Yes, but there is more to that house. Not just Glenda and a robot," continues Ham.

"How could that be?"

"There's more than one NeuNet microchip, plus hundreds of servers and devices in that house."

"You mean more than one Dreamscape user?" asks Kit.

"Exactly."

"Perhaps David Neumann, no?"

"Maybe. We'll have to check. But I also ran some AI analytics on the barcodes tattooed on Glenda's arm."

"And?"

"They look like encryption keys," the agent reveals.

"Good catch. Let's test those encryption keys," Kit directs firmly. "Ask your technical contact in Dreamscape to try them."

Chapter 106

Friday, August 19, 2050.
Dreamscape Office.

"What brings you guys here?" Roger gives Ham a quizzical look.

"Remember that list of locations that exchange encrypted data ... that none of your keys can open?" Agent Ham begins. "We have some encryption keys that we want you to test."

"I don't think that's possible," Roger shakes his head.

"Why not?"

"We are not authorized to decrypt any Dreamscape messages."

"What do you mean?"

"Subscription agreement. We have this agreement with each Dreamscape subscriber that we will maintain their privacy in Dreamscape."

He adds, "We run the risk of losing our business if our subscribers ever find out."

"You don't understand," Agent Jones butts in.

"I just do what I am told."

Then, Roger offers, "Or you can talk to our CEO, Don Goldman."

Chapter 107

Monday, August 22, 2050, 10AM.
Dreamscape Headquarters.

FBI Director Will Bridges enters the office of Dreamscape CEO, Don Goldman. Following strict Dreamscape protocols, Will wears a special mask and a pair of latex gloves before entering the spacious room at the penthouse of the NeuRoads Tower in New York City. It also serves as the headquarters of Dreamscape.

"Hi, Don. Good morning," Will Bridges greets the CEO.

Kit Sharper and a raft of agents wait in the board room, which is connected to Don's office using telepresence technologies.

Will extends his hand for a handshake.

"Have a seat," Don gestures to the FBI Director, completely ignoring Will's greetings and handshake offer.

"So, what is the FBI's interest?" asks Don.

"Let me go straight to the point," Bridges leans forward. "Where is Uri Borstin?"

"Do you have a warrant?"

"Not yet."

"Then I don't have to answer your questions. You're wasting my time."

"Mr. Goldman, one of your top investors was abducted. We suspect that Uri Borstin may have had something to do with it."

"That's not possible."

"Do you want us to bring this top investor to talk to you?"

"No. I don't think that will be necessary."

"So, back to Uri. Where is he?"

"Most of my employees work remotely. I don't keep track of them," the CEO intones, "and I don't like face-to-face meetings like this one we are having."

"Uri Borstin reports to you directly, correct?" asks Kit Sharper.

"Yes."

"How did you get to know Uri?" Kit Sharper probes.

"We constantly search for topnotch talents in the market. We hired him 15 years ago to design and develop the NeuNet technologies."

"He also designed the NeuNet microchip?"

"He was the Chief Architect of that technology."

"Your system does not have any record of Uri Borstin except his home address?" Kit sounds doubtful.

"We are only required by law to keep personnel records for five years. We also purge personally identifiable information upon the request of any employee," explains Don.

"Who supervises Uri Borstin's work?" Will Bridges rejoins the questioning.

"No one. Uri is highly dependable, a self-starter, and does not need any supervision," Don explains.

"You don't talk to Uri?"

"Uri's focus is technology. As CEO, I deal with the financials of the company."

Agent Ham joins in, "We found out that there are data packets moving inside Dreamscape that none of your encryption keys can open."

"What do you mean?" asks Don, trying not to look concerned.

"Someone is using Dreamscape to receive and transmit data ... using the Dreamscape network ... data that cannot be read by anyone else, not even your own technical people," the agent reveals.

Don's reply, "We don't read people's messages in Dreamscape. We are bound by contracts with all our subscribers that we will protect their privacy."

"We have some encryption keys that we want your team to try," Agent Ham looks the CEO in the eye.

"No. I won't authorize that," Don responds with a bit of edge to his voice. "It's against our subscription contract. We will lose our business."

"I don't think you understand, Mr. Goldman," Director Bridges counters.

"With all due respect, Mr. Bridges, you are the one who does not understand," Don says heatedly. "I am accountable to my customers and Board of Directors. Me. Not you!"

"We have reason to believe that an organization called Rainwater is using Dreamscape to receive and transmit data using special encryption," Will Bridges slips in the telling info.

"Rainwater?"

"Rainwater is a charity organization. On the surface. They give out free bottled water to poor people across many countries," Will explains.

"Nothing wrong with that," Don argues.

"Their water is contaminated with a compound that causes numerous neurologic disorders. They are killing people!" Will looks at Don in the eye.

"If you do not cooperate," his tone is firm, "we will be forced to charge you with obstruction of justice."

Don Goldman pauses to weigh his options.

Chapter 108

Monday, August 22, 2050, 11:45AM.
Dreamscape Global Command Center.

"We have some encryption keys that we want you to try," Agent Ham gets straight to the point.

"We know. Don told us," Tech lead Roger Dekalb is on his guard. "Let me call Siva Raja."

Siva walks towards the Fed agent and greets him.

"Remember those encrypted data that none of your keys could open?" Ham reminds him. "Here are some encryption keys that just might work."

With a few keystrokes, Siva is able to make readable messages suddenly appear on his screen. He rests on his seat, his mouth open in awe.

"Wow. Where did you get these encryption keys?" he asks wide-eyed.

"Why?"

"They work! So, who gave them to you?"

"Can't tell you. Can you decrypt the messages that were transmitted and received within the last 30 days across the locations that you gave me?" Ham asks.

"That's a lot of data."

"I know."

"Give me two days."

Chapter 109

Friday, August 26, 2050, 10:00AM Eastern Time.
FBI Director's Office.

"I reviewed the messages sent and received in the last 30 days across the multiple locations suspected to be operating under Rainwater," Ham reports excitedly.

"It's clear that Uri Borstin is operating from Ithaca, the house of Glenda Terrain. Uri constantly communicates with two people in Paris: Juliette LeMont and a certain Dima."

"Who is Dima?" asks Director Bridges.

"That must be Dmitri Borstin, the younger brother of Uri Borstin," says Jones.

"It is likely that Dmitri was one of the abductors that Rich Willard saw in Paris," Lee joins in.

Will Bridges points at Kit. "Send a report to the French about our persons of interest."

Then, "Carry on, Ham."

"Uri Borstin operates with hundreds of high-speed servers from Ithaca. He monitors and controls all Rainwater robots, automated water bottling equipment, driverless trucks, cars, drones, you name it."

"How can one man do all these?" asks Will Bridges.

"Artificial Intelligence," Agent Ham explains. "Uri Borstin built AI algorithms that think and act like humans, like his own clones."

Director Bridges barks, "Let's go and pay Uri Borstin a visit."

Chapter 110

Friday, August 26, 2050, 3:00PM Eastern Time.
1205 Base Line Road, Ithaca, New York.

Ten FBI flying vehicles quietly land around the perimeter at 1205 Base Line Road in Ithaca, New York.

Armed to the teeth, 32 men get out of their cars and swiftly surround the house.

Suddenly, ten humanoid soldiers appear out of nowhere and attack the Fed agents.

Three agents are immediately wounded and a furious exchange of gunfire ensues. The humanoids are far more agile than the Feds anticipated.

After a long fierce exchange of bullets, the robots are subdued by an EMP type weapon that shreds their electronics.

Chapter 111

Friday, August 26, 2050.
1205 Base Line Road, Ithaca, New York.

Agents sprint toward the entrance of the house and take covering positions.

The first man uses a battering ram to break down the door and the rest follow into the breach.

David Neumann suddenly comes running around the corner and is violently pinned to the ground by an agent who was a linebacker in college.

Agent Jones screams in his ear, "Where is Uri Borstin!?"

"He is not here," comes the muffled reply.

"Don't lie to us."

"What has he done?"

"Where is he?!!!"

"Ahhhhh!!!" David shouts in pain.

A section of the house's wall suddenly cracks open and out comes a barrage of bullets from high-caliber machine guns.

The agents closest to the wall visibly blanch, eyes frantically searching for whatever cover there is in the room but they know they are not going to make it.

Out of the corner of his eye from underneath the agent, Neumann sees the guns activate. He shouts as loud as he can, "Don't shoot!!" and with a whimper adds, "They are friends."

As soon as he says this, the guns stop tracking the agents and fold back up into their hidden recess.

The agents come out of hiding.

Upon realizing that Neumann is not the enemy, the former linebacker releases his grip on David.

"What the fuck was that?!" exclaims Agent Jones, trying to shake off his edgy nerves.

Chapter 112

Friday, August 26, 2050.
1205 Base Line Road, Ithaca, New York.

Another group of agents rush down the stairs leading to the basement.

The door is unlocked, like somebody is inviting them to come in.

They are not prepared for the sight that greets them.

A man in a white gown reclines on a hospital bed. Stuporous. Countless wires connect him to gleaming machines that keep him alive. He drools sporadically with intermittent spots of blood.

Floor-to-ceiling monitors cover the entire wall facing the foot of the bed. They are glowing and humming with high activity. One of the giant monitors shows a map of the world. It is filled with millions of colored dots.

Agent Ham senses that he is seeing a smaller version of the Dreamscape Global Command Center.

Without warning, four corners of the ceiling slide open and expose a raft of automatic weapons ready to perforate the mortal bodies of the Federal agents.

But a voice belays their execution.

For a few seconds, only the faint whirring of a respirator breaks the silence. Then, a modulated voice fills the frigid air.

"What took you so long, FBI agents?" a disembodied voice hisses, half-sneering.

The FBI agents look around to see where the voice is coming from.

"Uri Borstin," Jones declares quietly. His tone was more one of dread rather than relief. The mixed feeling of cheating death minutes ago and now chatting with Uri Borstin leaves him exhausted yet energized that everything might soon be coming to a reveal.

"Ah, you know my name, Agent Jones," the voice shifts to a relaxed tone. "I'm flattered."

"How do you know my name?" Jones asks.

"I have been tracking you in and out of Dreamscape. Everything that you did, all your conversations."

"How?" asks Jenny Lee, kind of miffed.

"The NeuNet microchip behind your ears. I designed that chip, including the ones issued to the Feds. I have access to all that you do. I have access to six billion users!"

"Shit! Our security had been breached!" The Fed agents are alarmed by their sudden realization.

Sensing his imminent finale, Uri unwraps another surprise. "I have been selling your intels to the highest bidders!"

"You'll go to prison!" Jones exclaims.

"Jones, you can't scare a dying person!"

"Don Goldman," Jones quips, changing the topic. "You report to him. Does he know what you do?"

"All that Goldman cares about is his money. He thinks I report to him. I let him think he is in control of NeuNet ... Dreamscape ... but the reality is that I ... I control ... I control all of it! All of it!" the voice declares exultantly.

"You are insane," Agent Lee quips.

"Insane? Genius is the appropriate term, Agent Jenny Lee," the voice proudly exclaims.

"How did you test your software codes?"

"I worked with Glenda Terrain."

"But Glenda is in coma," Agent Jones sputters incredulously.

"I knew I had a breakthrough when I was able to talk to Glenda in Dreamscape. Genius. Remember that, Agent Lee."

"You kidnapped Rich Willard and his daughter Margie. Why?"

Chapter 113

No one notices the absence of David Neumann who escaped through a secret passage amidst the wild commotion.

He is next seen in the back alley of his Syracuse apartment getting out of a flying car.

David contacts Dmitri, "They got your brother."

He cuts to the chase. "We go to Plan B. Now. I'll meet you there."

Dmitri Borstin grabs Juliette's hand.

He points a device to a spot behind her right ear. The NeuNet microchip is deactivated. A chip the size of a single rice pearl magically attaches to the wand.

Juliette does the same to Dmitri.

She hands the microchips to him, and he inserts the chips into a custom-built micro incinerator that Uri designed and developed many years ago ... for this very purpose. Plan B.

"Let's go," Dmitri says quietly as they board a black flying car and speed off.

Chapter 114

Friday, August 26, 2050.
1205 Base Line Road, Ithaca, New York.

"Oh, Rich-o Willard! Ha! He thinks he is God's gift to mankind," the voice turns angry.

"Rich Willard is an arrogant piece of shit, a delusional freak who thinks he is the most successful human being ... when all he did was inherit wealth from his parents."

"You know what he told me when we were in Columbia? He said, 'Go back to your home country. We don't need you here, you slimy pig!' What a fucking idiot! I was born here in America! Fuck you, racist!

"Willard and his cohorts are nothing but bullies who pick on people for sheer fun. He made my life in grad school miserable, all those put downs and snide remarks.

"It's time someone teaches him a lesson he will never forget. Rich thinks that he can just push people around. He thinks he can have anyone he wants. He has everything ... and yet ... he goes after Juliette ... my brother's wife!!!" the voice explodes in anger.

"Who is your brother?" Jones asks, overwhelmed.

"Go ahead. Play dumb, Agent Jones! Agent Lee knows the answer. She's the intelligent one among you," Borstin sneers.

"Dmitri Borstin," Lee says almost matter-of-factly.

"Good answer, Jenny," Borstin heckles.

"Dmitri was adopted before he turned one. Became Robert Devall. He will always be my brother Dima," adds Uri, suddenly emotional.

"Rainwater. You are Rainwater," Yoder blurts out.

"You get 90 points for that, Agent Yoder. What else do you know about my organization? Tell me."

"The water that you donate is laced with a deadly contaminant," Yoder recklessly retorts.

"Who told you that?!"

"The French Intelligence."

"See? The French are sharp!" Then, the voice turns cold. "You want to know why I do it?!"

"Why do you kill people?" Lee challenges.

"As you can see, I am dying, Agent Lee. The best legacy I can leave behind is a better world. Half of the world lives on dole outs. WorldGov extorts Bits from half of the population that is productive ... in order to support the other half. It's time to get rid of the non-performing humans!" Uri exclaims with conviction.

Then Uri adds in a calm and confident tone, "I will save humanity. The next generation will call me a hero!"

"What do you have against the poor?" Jones went for broke.

"I don't hate the poor. Poor is different from lazy. Bums!! You know what bums do? They beat their children ... my lazy ... my good-for-nothing stepdad ... he beat me ... every day ... every freaking day!"

Chapter 115

Somewhere in Paris.

With two leather duffel bags, a suitcase, three bags of groceries, and two NeuNet microchips that will give them new identities, Dmitri and Juliette board a flying car and take off towards the east.

They know exactly what Plan B means. They have repeatedly tested this disaster recovery plan many times in the past. Like a fire drill.

They switch from flying to driving on highways to ensure that they dodge any French police tracking device. They have made some costly customizations on their vehicle such that it changes color and license plates at the push of a hidden button.

A weird mix of severe anxiety and excitement grips the couple, knowing that they could be caught any time. A successful escape, though, would mean a peaceful life ahead of them.

Chapter 116

Friday, August 26, 2050.
1205 Base Line Road, Ithaca, New York.

The robotic weapons continue to track the agents who realize that there is no way in hell they could outrun smart bullets fired by advanced AI-guided weapons. Borstin continues to rant and is getting increasingly agitated by the second.

"Three years ago, we asked Rich Willard for donations. You know what he told us?"

"Charity is for the weak and lazy," Agent Lee offers.

"What an arrogant asshole!" shouts Uri Borstin.

"You are no different from Rich Willard!" Agent Lee takes a huge risk.

"What did you just say?!

"You realize, Lee, that the population of this world has reached 12 billion and there is no way that this world can support that many people without putting humanity in peril," Borstin is adamant. "At least I am doing something about it."

"Right. By selling our intels and blackmailing people," Lee quips.

"The end justifies the means. People who don't produce—and who leach off the ones willing to work—do not serve any useful purpose."

"So, this is your smart solution?" Lee bristles. "Giving them poisoned water so they can ... can literally choke on it?!"

"Most of them are bums who choose not to have a purpose in life ... zombies ... they walk around like us, but they are actually already dead!"

"You are a monster!" Jones seethes with disgust.

Uri Borstin pauses for a moment, choosing the words he is going to say next. And they come like a bolt of lightning.

"I wonder if monster also applies to you, Agent Jones, when you sent a stalking surveillance drone to that rando you mistakenly thought was giving your fiancé the eye. You might think that an FBI agent would have the wherewithal to first get the facts straight, but no!"

Borstin screams in a taunting tone, "You almost joyfully went for a messy kill!"

"That's not true!" shouts Jones.

"Really? Don't deny. I have been listening. In fact, let me play back your conversations!" Borstin ends sneeringly.

Lee instantly senses the animosity of the other agents who heard everything. By training, she instinctively goes for Jones's sidearm.

That was the last thing Jenny Lee ever did, as a hail of metal cuts through her left shoulder. Another agent's lifeless body is hurled against the opposite wall with the sheer force of the projectiles.

As the other agents rush to the stairs, Jones dives toward the bed where Borstin is lying, hoping against hope that the intelligent weapons would spare their primary control. But a smart bullet misses Jones, hits Borstin's temple, and splatters his brain against the pillow.

In the room where Glenda lies, the agents are back in the fight of their lives as the nursing droids suddenly wield firearms and shoot. With no David to stop them, the armed humanoids go berserk.

A bullet hits Ham's right leg and he drops to the floor writhing. He manages to hang on to his sidearm and hits a droid, knocking it out of commission. Two more agents are seriously wounded before Yoder hurls an EMP grenade and puts a stop to the rampage.

Another agent makes his way to Glenda's bed to secure her but the EMP flash-bang fries the circuits of the machines that are keeping her alive. She flatlines almost instantly.

In the basement, the monitors on the walls brighten up. Lines appear on all the monitors, almost like the whole system is cleaning up.

A robotic voice intones sans emotion, "Commencing self-destruction in 10 seconds ... Nine ... Eight ... Seven ... Six ... Five ... Four ... Three ... Two ... One."

A split second after, sparks shoot out of the walls and a raging fire starts to engulf the whole house.

The surviving agents drag the wounded up the basement stairs and scamper to put as much real estate between their bleeding bodies and the house.

They are not a couple of dozen yards away when the whole house implodes and collapses to the ground.

Agents Jones, Lee, Yoder, and Ham look at each other in disbelief as they lie heaving on the grass.

Minutes later, fire trucks and police cars arrive at the scene.

Chapter 117

Monday, August 29, 2050, 7:00PM.
House of the Willards.

"This is your evening news. I am Diane Tobin and these are the headlines: Don Goldman steps down as CEO of NeuRoads Corporation ..."

"Did you hear that, honey?" asks Emily as she turns to Rich who is walking away from the living room.

"Am sure that they will find a replacement soon."

"I hope so. Didn't we bet big on Dreamscape?"

"Hmm. Not too big. Won't put us in the doghouse," Will remarks almost haughtily as he goes up the stairs.

Chapter 118

Juliette LeMont holds a newborn baby boy.

"He looks so much like you, Robert."

Dmitri smiles as he looks down at his firstborn child.

"Simple man with a simple life, that is what he will be," Dmitri muses as they gaze at the wide expanse of farmland surrounding their hideaway.

A flying car silently sets down.

Out comes David Neumann, smiling from ear to ear.

Our special thanks to the following people who helped turn this book from vision to reality: Melissa Moran for superb editing, Stephen Simon for the awesome book cover design, and to our dearest friends, Henry Garcia, Cindy Garcia, Elzar Simon, and Elisa Simon.

About the Authors:

William Scott Hill has spent time in both halves of the globe. Having lived and worked, while raising a family, first in Sydney then New York, he calls California home, for now. A seasoned techie fellow, he is both amazed and alarmed at the speed the world is hurtling towards a future you may, or may not want to be in. When he is not writing, he does a brill James Taylor ... both in singing and guitar playing.

Jack Horner lives in a small Midwest town with his wife and an attack dog, a golden doodle who really just has to kiss everyone. When Jack takes a break from the keyboard, he is out walking Milo in all kinds of weather. He has since lost a lot of weight.